ALL THE THINGS WE NEVER KNEW

LIARA TAMANI

ALL THE THINGS WE NEVER KNEW

Greenwillow Books
An Imprint of HarperCollins*Publishers*

The text of this book is set in Garamond. Book design by Sylvie Le Floc'h

Library of Congress Cataloging-in-Publication Data

Names: Tamani, Liara, author.
Title: All the things we never knew / Liara Tamani.
Description: First edition. | New York, NY : Greenwillow Books, an imprint of HarperCollinsPublishers, [2020] | Audience: Ages 13 up. | Audience: Grades 10-12. | Summary: "Carli and Rex have an immediate connection, an understanding that must mean first love, but family secrets, disappointments—and basketball, which holds center stage in both their lives—all create complications"—Provided by publisher.
Identifiers: LCCN 2019060207 | ISBN 9780062656919 (hardback) | ISBN 9780062656933 (ebook)
Subjects: CYAC: Dating (Social customs)—Fiction. | Basketball—Fiction. | Family life—Texas—Fiction. | African Americans—Fiction. | Texas—Fiction.
Classification: LCC PZ7.1.T355 All 2020 | DDC [Fic]—dc23
LC record available at https://lccn.loc.gov/2019060207

20 21 22 23 24 PC/LSCH 10 9 8 7 6 5 4 3 2 1

First Edition

 Greenwillow Books

For anyone who's ever wanted love from someone in pain

"Love is never any better than the lover."
—Toni Morrison, *The Bluest Eye*

CONTENTS

THE
VERY
FIRST
KISSES

 CARLI

Nobody ever warned me about love. Nobody ever warned me that when the greatest thing in the world hits you too hard, too fast, the blast can crush the organs in your belly, send heat flying up the right side of your face, and make your heart forget how to beat normally.

I'm trying to stay in my body, on the sidelines of the gym, but the pain in my belly is making the sound of the bouncing basketball grow fainter. The fluorescent lights keep giving way to darkness.

The boy is the only one who can see the pain. The boy at the free-throw line in his high socks with his high-top fade and his inverted triangle face, drenched with tenderness. The boy who just came out of nowhere, blowing me a kiss in the middle of his game. Who even blows kisses these days? But it wasn't corny like you'd think. It came from somewhere deep, like all of his years and hurts and hopes were attached to it—his whole history.

And now our histories are mixing.

Pain on high, feeling like I'm about to die, an old fact flickers at the front of my mind:

The very first kisses were blown in Mesopotamia as a way to get in good with the gods.

Tacked that up on my bedroom wall after Bradley Dixon blew me a kiss in the fifth grade. The next day he told everyone the kiss wasn't meant for me.

The boy drops the basketball at the free-throw line and runs toward me, just off the court.

Darkness briefly takes me, but the sharp sound of a whistle blown scares the darkness away. I bite some skin peeling on my bottom lip and try to stay in the gym. Keep my focus on him.

He's wearing number twelve—ten less than the number on the jersey underneath my warm-ups. I need to take off these stupid polyester pants, this jacket. I'm burning up, drenched in sweat. Zipper. Where's the zipper? My fingers fumble to find it, but the pain . . . the darkness . . . I can't fight it anymore. I'm losing myself to it . . . falling.

His arms around me, and my insides light up with his down-slanted, hooded eyes. It feels so good the way they're staring into mine. For a second I've never felt so alive. Then I'm gone.

● REX ●

I miss a shot. An easy shot. My mid-range jumper always drops. Always. But man, I can't stop thinking about that girl. About how she passed out in my arms. How, for a second, I thought she might've been dead, and it was somehow my fault.

I was so scared I started crying. I didn't even stop when I saw her chest rising. Rising and falling, again and again, underneath her royal-blue warm-ups. It took four whole breaths for my eyes to convince my head of what my heart was afraid to trust. Good thing my back was to everyone else.

"Carli!" her team's trainer called out, running onto the court. She was a tiny woman, five feet at best. "Lay her down flat on the floor," she ordered with a steady downward motion of her right arm.

I did what I was told.

"Carli!" she shouted again, and lifted Carli's legs up about twenty degrees.

Kneeling beside Carli, I leaned in close and said her name for the first time, feeling the *ar* wobble in my throat.

"Back up, back up," the trainer yelled at me. "Give her some space!"

She could hang that up. I wasn't going anywhere. I reached down and scraped Carli's big, sweaty hair off the sides of her face. Even in a ponytail, it was everywhere. I was about to say her name again—

"I said back up!" the trainer yelled, like I can only imagine a mama would after she's repeated herself for the last time and you'd better listen this time if you know what's good for you.

I stood, backed up, and Carli's eyelashes fluttered like she didn't want me to leave. But the rest of her team immediately crowded me out. I stayed close, though, looking over the tops of their heads, watching her eyes tremble and go still.

The trainer waved something under her nose that made her eyes open wide, but only for a second. Then the paramedics came and rolled her out on a stretcher.

I hope she's okay. She has to be okay, right? They wouldn't let us keep playing if she wasn't okay. Right?

"Hustle back! Hustle back!" Coach Bell shouts, running up the sideline, swinging his short arm in a wide circle.

Twenty-eight seconds left in the game and it's tied 71–71. *Focus, Rex,* I tell myself, and sprint back. We can't lose to Gaines and let them get their confidence up. They'll be our biggest competition at the state championship, only five weeks out. We gotta shut these boys down now.

I'm coming up behind their point guard, Russell Price. Can't stand this dude. He thinks he's so much better than he actually is. He dribbles the ball between his legs—once . . . twice . . . three times—trying to look cool. Then he tries to pass to his shooting guard, but the pass is lazy and slow.

Thanks, I'll take that. I steal the ball and sprint back up the left side of court. Out of the corner of my eye, I see Russell coming up behind me on my right. *You ain't slick.* I switch the ball to my left hand so he can't steal it back. The crowd is chanting, "Rex! Rex! Rex!" Nearing the basket, I cross back to my right, leap, and cock the ball back for a nasty dunk. But Russell tackles me hard to the ground.

"Number-one player my ass," he says, still on top of me.

With the back of my head and tailbone throbbing, I

quickly shove Russell off of me. All I want to do is get up and knock this fool out. I can almost feel my fist meeting his sweaty cheek, see his head whipping back over his right shoulder before he falls limp to the ground. But the referee blows his whistle and wakes me from my rage. Then he holds his fist in the air and signals for two regular foul shots.

"What?" I shout, and quickly hop up to protest the call. "It should've been a flagrant!"

Coach Bell agrees. He's on the sideline yelling, "Flagrant!" and banging his forearms together in an X above his head.

The crowd is booing in agreement, too.

"If that wasn't a flagrant foul, I don't know what is!" I shout, walking behind the ref. "This ain't football. You can't tackle somebody like that."

But the ref ignores me.

"Man, this is some bullshit!" I yell at the back of the ref's balding head.

The ref immediately makes a hard T with his hands to signal a technical foul.

"Are you serious?" I shout, throwing up both of my arms.

Danny, our point guard, grabs me and pulls me away from the ref before I get another tech.

At the free-throw line, I calm down. This is exactly where Carli caught the kiss usually meant for Mom.

Wait, before you try to play me, blowing a kiss has been a part of my free-throw routine since I was eight and discovered Jason Kidd on YouTube. I figured if a ten-time NBA All-Star and two-time Olympic Gold Medal winner could blow kisses as part of his game and not be lame, then so could I.

Every time he went to the free-throw line, he blew a kiss, took one dribble, and shot. To tell his wife and kids he loved them. Every time I go to the line, I blow a kiss, take three dribbles, and shoot. To tell Mom I'm sorry.

But today, Carli was there instead. And I swear it was like she was a gift straight from Mom. See, I pray to Mom every day. Figure she should have some clout, hanging with the celestial bodies and all.

And for the longest, I've been praying she'd send someone my way who could really see me. Not like these girls out here flashing cute smiles, trying to get at me because of how I ball. Or even the genuine ones I can't make myself feel anything for.

The way Carli looked at me was like she could feel the deepest parts of me. The soft parts. The parts that nobody sees. Man, her look pushed up against me so hard that something inside me shook loose and started falling. I was scared. But the way Carli's dark brown eyes stared into mine told me something inside her was falling, too. I'm telling you nothing has ever felt so good.

Focus, Rex. With everyone lined up around the key, the ref passes me the ball. I blow a kiss, dribble three times, and shoot, like always. But I can't help looking beyond the rim, remembering Carli's eyes dimming, her long body going limp.

The ball misses everything.

Damn.

And to make matters worse, the crowd starts chanting, "Air ball . . . air ball."

Another chance, another kiss, another three dribbles, another air ball, and another stupid chant from the crowd.

From half-court, I watch Russell Price shoot the technical fouls. And make them. *Great, just great.*

Fifteen seconds left. Gaines gets the ball back. Their point guard inbounds to Russell. *Can't let this dude score on top of everything else.* I get in my best defensive stance—legs and arms wide and ready. He fakes left and tries to drive to the basket, but I stay in front of him and stop him. He pulls up to shoot, but I put a hand in his face, and he misses. I block him out, grab the rebound, and dribble up the court.

Five seconds. Two points down.

I fake right and go left past two defenders. I'm at

the three-point line, within shooting range.

Three seconds.

A couple more steps to get a higher probability shot.

One second.

With Russell's hands in my face, trying to block the ball, I shoot.

Looks like it's going in, but the ball hits the inside of the rim—*fall, please fall*—and bounces out.

The whole Gaines team and their fans descend upon center court, jumping and cheering.

We just lost the tournament. To Matthew Gaines High. And it's my fault. I should be pissed. I should feel like taking the basketball and drop-kicking it across the gym. But instead, I'm standing here thinking about Carli . . . remembering her face . . . hoping she's okay.

CARLI

The hospital room door flies open and my brother Cole rushes in with way too much excitement.

"Dude! Do you know who that was?"

I stare at him wide-eyed, like he's gone crazy—my default expression for watching his fits of excitement. Boy is prone to having at least one a day.

"Rex Carrington! You managed to pass out in the arms of *the* Rex Carrington!"

The name sounds familiar, but I can't place it. "Okaaay."

"Do you really not know who Rex Carrington is? He only holds the record for the most points scored in a Texas high school basketball game. Ever. Like, in the history of the world. And he's only a junior! He's ESPN's high school player of the year, for Christ's sake!"

"Wait, are you talking about that boy Daddy calls the next LeBron? I thought he went to Yates."

"Yes, him! He moved to Woodside this year. And look! I found a video of him catching you," he says, and pulls his iPhone from his pocket.

Of course, Cole thinks he's king of the Internet. But do I thank the king and kindly ask him to hurry up because I'm about to lose my mind in anticipation of seeing the boy's face again?

No.

Do I obey the urge surging through my body to squeal with glee?

Absolutely not.

The title of the YouTube video is "Rex Carrington to the Rescue!" Come on, could it get any cheesier? Cole presses Play and I stare at the screen, hoping to get a glimpse of the boy's face as he blew me a kiss. But the camera angle is behind him, and whoever made the video started late. So there's only me and my frizzy red hair, collapsing in his arms, looking all damsel-in-distress dramatic. "Uh, cut it off," I moan.

"What? It's brilliant!" Cole says.

"It doesn't even have the part where he blew me the kiss," I complain, and eye my dinner menu, still on the hospital tray beside the bland chicken, white rice, and pale, limp broccoli I picked at. On the back of it, I'd written:

The very first kisses were blown in Mesopotamia as a way to get in good with the gods.

Until I get home and unearth the original from my bedroom wall, it'll have to do. That fact, together with Rex's kiss, has to be a sign, right?

"Blew you a kiss?" Cole asks.

"Yeah, they didn't catch it on the video, but Rex blew me a kiss while he was standing at the free-throw line."

"No, that's part of his free-throw routine."

"The kiss?"

"Yeah, he blows a kiss every time he goes to the line," Cole says, and snaps a picture of me.

"Come on, Cole. You know I'm rough," I whine.

"You're beautiful," he says, and takes another pic— always his response.

"Anyway, I'm telling you, Rex blew *me* a kiss. I mean, he was looking dead at me."

"Oh, I see. You wanted him to blow you a kiss."

"No, I'm just stating the facts."

"Look, all I know is that he always blows a kiss before his free throws. It's, like, his thing. I think he does it for good luck or something. I don't know, but he's been doing it for years."

Everything I thought me and Rex had crumples into a hard ball. *I swear I'm so stupid.*

But it was so real. The way he looked at me. It was like he was offering himself up. His whole, tender self. And I wrapped myself in him, my heart bleeding color.

"Oh, snap. You like him, don't you?" Cole says, staring at me, every freckle on his face ready to bust out doing backflips. He doesn't have nearly as many as Daddy and me, but still.

I sit up a little straighter in the hospital bed, trying to

regain some of my dignity. "Boy, please. I don't even know that boy like that."

He eyes me down, hunting for the lie. I swear Cole is a romance junkie. Had what he calls his first serious relationship in the second grade. Had a two-year run with Alexis in the fourth and fifth grades. For the past five years, seems like he's had a new girl on his screensaver every month. And according to him, they've all been the real thing.

A few knocks on the open door, and a lady pushing a big, silver cart walks in. She has on way too much foundation, and it doesn't quite match the beige of her face. "Done with your food?" she asks.

I look down at the tray, thinking about the other side of the menu. About the first kisses fact. About the things I feel but won't admit. It doesn't seem right letting this lady with bad makeup roll it away.

She opens the door to the cart, exposing a stack of trays with half-eaten food.

Well, it's definitely not going in there. "Yeah, I'm done. Thanks," I say. And while Cole is busy getting out of the lady's way, I quickly grab the menu and tuck it underneath my right thigh. The kiss wasn't for me—fine!—but I still can't let the first sign of me and Rex's fate become hospital waste.

The lady slips the tray into an empty slot inside the cart and heads out.

Cole slides next to me and says, "So, back to you liking Rex."

"Whatever. Nobody's even thinking about that boy like that," I say, imagining the first kisses fact as a tattoo on the back of my thigh.

"Rex Carrington! His name is Rex Carrington!" he practically shouts.

"Give your sister a break, why don't you," Daddy tells Cole as he ducks under the doorframe. The doorframe actually looks taller than his reddish-brown fade by a few inches. But being six-foot-seven, he's had enough headbutting experiences to instinctively duck whenever it's a close call. He walks around to the other side of the bed and gives me a kiss on the cheek. His face, usually smooth, is rough with bright, patchy stubble. "How are you feeling, Angel-face?"

Angel-face? I haven't heard that name since I was, like, eight. Hospital or not, we are *not* about to revive *Angel-face.* "Not dying or anything," I answer. "Carli is still good."

"Got it," Daddy says, with a single nod of his head. "I spoke to the doctor in the hall. If we schedule the surgery soon, you could be back as early as two weeks."

Back home? I think. But the surgery isn't that serious.

Back to school? But that would be way too long. Then I realize he's talking about basketball. Of course, he's talking about basketball. He's always talking about basketball. "Yeah?" I reply, close my eyes, and pretend to be tired from all the drama of passing out.

I forgot to tell you about that. At the basketball tournament earlier today, I had a gallbladder attack. Yes, a gallbladder attack. Apparently, in rare cases, sixteen-year-olds can have them. Basically, the pain of a gall stone passing through my bile duct was so intense that it made me faint. And now the doctor says my gallbladder has to come out.

"Hey, Mom," Cole says.

I open my eyes and see Cole giving Mom a hug. Dang, he's so much taller than her now. I guess I'm taller than her, too—barely. Cole only passed her last year but has grown five inches since. Now he's almost catching Daddy. I swear the boy has gotten taller since dinner last night.

"Oh, did y'all win?" I ask Cole. He had a basketball tournament today, too. Caught up with all the gallbladder stuff, I'd forgotten to ask him about it. I try to be super supportive because he can get down on himself about still playing on JV. It's normal for sophomores to play on JV. Me making varsity three years ago as a freshman is not the norm.

Cole doesn't answer me. He's still hugging Mom. Cole

loves hugs—good-morning hugs . . . good-night hugs . . . happy-to-meet-you hugs . . . happy-to-see-you (even though I just saw you five minutes ago) hugs . . . sorry-you-had-to-spend-the-last-three-hours-detangling-your-hair hugs . . . sorry-you-spilled-water-all-over-your-magazine hugs. He lets go of Mom but still doesn't answer me. He's staring at her.

Mom walks over to me, and Daddy backs up toward the window. He doesn't speak to Mom and Mom doesn't speak to him. Mom's eyes are red and puffy, like she's been crying for a long time. Clearly, they've been fighting.

Mom pinches my big toe, poking up from underneath the thin hospital bedding, and briefly wiggles it around. Then she pats my left leg—shin, knee, thigh—as she walks closer to the head of the bed. "Gallbladder attack, huh?" she says. It's crazy; even with puffy eyes and no makeup, she's still beautiful.

"That's what they tell me," I say, staring at her. It's weird. She's my mom and I see her every day, but her beauty still strikes me all the time. She's tall and slim and has a teeny-weeny 'fro that makes her face, with its high cheekbones and thick lips and dark glowing skin, pop . . . even on what seems to be a sad, shitty day.

"Must be hereditary. I had to get mine removed in my late twenties."

"For real?" I say, and a forgotten memory of me running my fingers over a scar on her stomach rushes to the front of my brain. I was super young, probably like five.

"Yep, had a gallbladder attack when I was in New Orleans, furniture shopping for a client. Passed out in one of my favorite little antique shops. Had to get rushed to the hospital just like you, you know."

"No, we don't know. Why didn't you ever tell us about this?" Cole asks, but it sounds more like an accusation than a question. He's clearly still worried about Mom. The boy needs to relax.

Mom shrugs. "I don't know. Guess it never crossed my mind."

"While you're telling things, would you be so kind as to tell everyone what you decided today?" Daddy says in his lawyer voice. He goes from leaning on the windowsill to standing up straight, like he's readying himself to approach the witness. I hate when his lawyer side comes out . . . always acting like someone's on trial. But this is not the courtroom. We are not his clients. And Mom is not on the witness stand. He can save the drama for work.

Mom ignores him, not even turning around to look at him. When she's pissed, she doesn't curse or shout. She ignores.

And Daddy hates it. "Barbara, please answer the question." Now he's standing with his hands behind his back, in serious lawyer mode.

She turns around and gives him a look. "Derek, this is not the time or the place."

Cole walks around Mom and stands by the head of my bed. Mom and Daddy never fight like this in front of us. They save their fights for behind bedroom and car doors, mostly about Mom working so much.

I wonder if this is about her opening up that new boutique. It's going to be similar to the one already attached to her interior design offices, only bigger. It's been in the works for a while, but she's been waiting on the right time to tell Daddy. Cole doesn't know about it, either. Can't tell him anything unless you want the whole world to know.

"Barbara, you're the one who wants this. So go ahead and tell them." His emotions are starting to get the best of him and he's falling out of lawyer mode.

"For fuck's sake, can somebody please tell us what's going on," Cole exclaims, his voice super high and shaking all over the place.

No one corrects Cole about his language. Mom and Daddy are too busy staring each other down.

The door swings open. "Now that the whole gang is

here," Dr. Williams says, walking in, tossing her long gray locs over her shoulder. But she doesn't finish her sentence. She's noticing the tension in the room, and we're all noticing her notice the tension in the room. Can't get any more awkward. She looks down at her clipboard through her rectangular, red-framed glasses like she's reading something (she knows she's not reading anything) and looks back up.

Then she starts talking about the surgery. Yes, the surgery. That's what she's here to discuss—what the laparoscopic cholecystectomy (gallbladder removal surgery) will involve.

Four tiny incisions around my belly button.

A tiny video camera, which she will insert into my abdomen via one of the incisions.

A video monitor (not tiny), which will display the inside of my abdomen via the camera.

Surgical tools, which she will use to remove my gallbladder from my abdomen while watching the monitor.

Insane, right? But apparently it's no big deal. I should be able to leave the hospital a few hours after surgery. And I'll only take about two weeks to recover.

Daddy brings up the state championship, the fact that it's only five weeks away.

Mom and I trade glances.

Cole is staring at the TV, high up in the corner of the room, looking like he's about to cry.

Daddy wants to schedule the surgery for this Monday, as in the day after tomorrow.

The doctor brings up the necessary presurgery lab work.

Mom brings up school.

The surgery will be scheduled for this Friday.

I'm free to go. In the meantime, if I start feeling another attack coming on, I need to find somewhere to lie down so I don't hurt myself fainting. I was lucky this time.

REX

First thing I do when I get on the bus is head straight to the back. Doubt anyone wants to sit next to me. But to be safe, I take the very last seat, toss my backpack in the one across from me, put my headphones on, and arrange my face to match the mood I should be in.

Not only did Coach give us (really me) a thirty-minute locker-room speech about the need to focus, he made everybody make ten free throws in a row before we could get on the bus to go home. Mind you, it's a Saturday night, i.e., date night, and it's still gonna take us another forty-five minutes to get all the way back out to the boonies. Phones have been blowing up. Nya has already texted me twice.

But I'm not worried about any of that. All I want is some private time with Carli. I want to sit back, with no eyes over my shoulders, and find her on IG to make sure she's okay. Scroll through her pictures and stare at her face.

Josh, our backup small forward, walks up the aisle and eyes the seat across from me that I've clearly already claimed with my backpack.

No music playing yet, but I slide the left side of my headphones above my ear. "Nah, that's me," I tell him.

"Well, you're sitting over there. So which one is it?" he asks, hate smeared across his round, red-cheeked face. Dude *stays* trying to start some shit. He can't stand me because I took his starting position when I moved out here this year.

It's too bad for Josh. Heard he's been praying for a letter from Michigan State. But graduating this year with the playing time he's been getting, he'll be lucky if he gets to play at the YMCA. Jokes, but he probably won't be playing D1.

But what am I supposed to do? I have goals, too. Lofty-ass goals at that. Your boy is trying to be one-and-done.

"Dude, you got *all* these seats," I say, floating my extended arm across the width of the rumbling bus. All I need to add is *presentiiiing*. Thirteen rows, twelve players, two coaches who always share the first row, and one trainer. Josh *was* the last one to get on the bus. He'd better find the trainer and double up with him.

"But what if I really want *that* seat?" Josh says with a hard, directed nod of his big head.

A few players look back to see what's going on.

"You wanna sit beside me that bad, huh?"

Josh shoves his short, curly bangs away from his face. "Not as bad as I wanna kick your ass."

All I can do is laugh. This fool must think that because he has the body of a linebacker and I'm on the lean side that he could take me. Clearly, he doesn't know me. He doesn't know about all the scraps I've gotten into roaming the streets as a kid in my old neighborhood.

Josh walks off, throwing a weak "asshole" over his shoulder, and settles into a row toward the middle of the bus. The lights lower and the grumbling bus starts rolling.

Finally. I slide my left headphone back on, find

Khalid in Spotify, and snuggle up with Carli.

Ten minutes later, thanks to her brother's IG, I know Carli Renée Alexander is more than okay. Man, let me tell you. She's perfect. And she's in the hospital—not dead. It's not like I really thought she was dead or anything, but it's good to know she's alive and well. *And* I'm playing a game at her school in a week! Doubt she'll be there with the surgery and everything, but her brother is on the JV team, which plays right before our game. So I can give my number to him.

Twenty minutes later and I'm still digging. I'm not one of those crazy stalker dudes or anything. I just can't stop looking for new pictures of her face. She has this cute little button nose, sprinkled with freckles, and these dark brown eyes that pop out of her pale brown skin and take hold of me.

Man, I can't even tell you what I feel when I look at her face. It's better than stepping into an empty gym before the sun comes up. Better than walking through the pines after it rains and having a stray drop land on my nose. Better than thumbing through Mom's old poetry books, finding words I can feel. Or listening to her old records. Or staring at her old beetle collection. Looking at Carli's face, it's like I get lost to some kind of force. Sounds stupid, I know, but

I've never felt anything like it before. Anything *close*.

I look up to grab a Snickers bar out of my duffel bag and notice most of the team crowded around someone's seat toward the middle of the bus. I slide my headphones off and hear people cracking up.

"It must've been that big-ass afro," someone says in a low voice.

"He likes big 'fros and he cannot lie," someone else says in the rhythm of that old Sir Mix-a-Lot song.

Everyone laughs.

I think about Carli's big red hair, about Nya's natural puff. A knot forms in my chest and I stand up.

"Oh my gosh, Becky, look at her 'fro. It is so big. She looks like one of Rex's girlfriends," someone continues in the Valley girl accent from the song.

Everybody busts out laughing again.

More knots, pounding harder. It's not like it's the first time I've overheard my new teammates talking about me. I usually ignore it. But them bringing Carli and Nya into it is different. It's like all the air around me, the engine rumbling beneath me, everything inside me is begging me to shut it down.

As I walk down the aisle, I see a light coming from a seat. Closer, and I peep over our shooting guard's shoulder and see Carli passing out in my arms on Josh's phone..

Illuminated faces all around and I swear I want to knock the laughs right out of their mouths. Our point guard, Danny, kneeling on the seat in front of Josh, is laughing so hard he's in tears. Out of everyone, I thought he could've been my friend.

Leo, our backup point guard, sees me and elbows Danny. Danny looks up at me guiltily, turns around, and sits down.

Josh (of course it's Josh) continues in his Valley girl voice. "I can't believe it's just so round . . . it's like out there. I mean gross. Look, she's just so . . . black."

That does it. I reach over the back of the seat and snatch the phone out of his hand. "Say something else about my girl and your phone is as good as gone."

Someone says, "Oh shit," and everyone ducks off back to their seats.

Wait, did I just call Carli "my girl"?

The hard pounding in my chest answers with a thousand pissed-off yeses.

Josh stands up. "Give me back my phone!" he whines like he's five years old.

And my five-year-old self knows exactly how to

respond. "What phone?" I ask, and slide it into my right warm-up pocket.

"What's the big deal? I wasn't even talking about Nya. I was talking about that girl who passed out. It's not like you know that stupid girl."

The pounding in my chest shoots through the top of my head, and I can feel the last bit of my sense leaving me. I don't try to stop it. "So first you want to make fun of her hair and now you want to call her stupid?" I yell. "Oh, you gon' learn today!" I march back to my seat, feeling Josh close behind me. When I get there, I squeeze the latches on the window and pull it down—cold air rushing in.

"You better stop playing, Rex! Give me back my phone!"

The cold air slapping me in the face gives me a rare glimpse of my anger. He's like the homie from way-back-when who always has my back but chronically takes shit too far. But what am I supposed to do now? Back down from Josh? Nah. I grab his phone out of my pocket and hold it out of the window.

Everyone gasps. They're all turned around, kneeling on their seats, staring at who they think they see. The asshole who acts like he's too good to talk to anybody or hang with anybody. But it's not even like that. Not even close.

"What the hell is going on back there?" Coach Bell finally gets up and yells.

Everyone sits down and faces forward in their seats.

It takes a lot for Coach to intervene on the bus. It's the one place he completely removes himself. In the name of team bonding, the one place we get to make up our own rules, settle our own disputes.

"Rex is trying to throw my phone out of the window!" Josh answers, his five-year-old self back in full effect.

My five-year-old self wants to yell *Snitch!* But I don't let him, not in front of Coach.

"Have you lost your mind?" Coach shouts down the aisle. "Give Josh his phone back."

I pull my arm back in and toss the phone on the seat.

Josh grabs it and storms off.

"Rex, do I need to treat you like you're my child and make you come sit up here with me?" Coach yells.

A simple rhetorical question, but it shoots deep, pricking the place I'm always pushing further down inside of me. It's just that the words *my child* make me want to answer *yes*. I swear I'm so pathetic.

WHERE
IT
HURTS

CARLI

When I get home, Cole's in my room, sitting on my floor, still in his basketball warm-ups. He's leaning against my bed, surrounded by a ton of old photos. Him and Daddy left the hospital right after the doctor left the room. Mom and I had to wait over an hour for my discharge papers. Looks like Cole's been in here the whole time.

"Hey," I say.

"Hey," he replies, but doesn't look up from a photo he's holding.

I head to my desk, where I remember tacking up the fact about ancient kisses, and look for it underneath a magazine clipping of a guitarfish. Not there. A charcoal sketch of Mom doing a backbend. Nope. A card of a young girl—eyes closed, hugging a book to her chest, with castles and dinosaurs and ships and cities and birds and trees in her curly afro. Not there, either.

"We have to choose," Cole says.

I look over at him, and his eyes are red. He's definitely been crying. But Cole cries at least once every couple of weeks, so I'm not too worried. Still, I stop my search after one last look under a crayon picture of a dark sea.

Then I tiptoe around all of Cole's photos to the corner of the room where my bed is.

"We have to choose," he repeats, and hands me a picture as I climb onto my bed.

I cross my legs and look down at the photo. I've never seen it before but remember Cole taking it. We were on the suspension bridge at the Bayou Bend Gardens a few years ago. While Mom, Daddy, and I waited in the middle of the bridge, Cole pushed the timer on the camera he'd set up and ran to get in place.

"Cute," I say, looking at Daddy's long arm draped around Mom and my head in the crux of Cole's elbow, one leg up in the air like I'm about to fall over. Real smiles all around. I hand it back to him.

"Did you hear what I said? We have to choose." He rips

the photo in half—Mom and I on one side, him and Daddy on the other.

"Really, Cole?" I swear he can't get any more dramatic. "You might as well give it to me now." I scan my walls for the perfect place to fit the photo. *There*, I think, spotting the winged Greek goddess, Solange of Samothrace (I gave the Nike sculpture Solange's head, and in my mind, she thanked me), right above my closet. The Bayou Bend Gardens has a cool collection of Greek goddess statues. The picture will feel at home there.

"Listen," he says, and places the half of the picture with him and Daddy down beside his long, outstretched legs. "Dad's moving out."

The words come at me so straight it's hard to register them. "Wait. What?"

Then he places the half with Mom and me on the other side of his legs. "They're getting divorced."

"Huh?" I wish he would slow down. He's not making any sense.

Cole turns to face me. "Look, Mom and Dad are getting divorced, and we have to choose who we want to live with."

My insides start plummeting. I feel like a baby fish who just got dropped out of a plane. A baby fish who's flapping her fins in foreign air, trying to stay afloat, but keeps falling faster and faster. I read about it in *National Geographic* last night. About how some states repopulate their lakes by farming fish until they reach a certain age and then they release them into the wild by dropping them out of planes. After hitting the water, 90 percent of them survive. But I don't know if I'll survive. I can't take this new reality Cole is dumping me into. "Will you wait a second!"

But Cole's not listening. "If we choose Dad, we go to a new school. He's not sure where yet, but somewhere closer to his job." His voice is so even, so unemotional, like he's not even talking about our life, our parents, our family. "We'll get to see the parent we don't choose every other weekend."

"This is our life you're talking about!" I yell. Something breaks behind my eyes, and tears rage down my face. Strange, warm tears. It's been so long since I've felt them.

"I know," he says, without trying to give me a hug. He's still so calm. It's like we've switched places and I'm the emotional wreck and he's the chill one. What the hell's going on? I am *not* supposed to be like this. He is *not* supposed to be like this. This is *not* supposed to be happening.

I scoot fast to the edge of the bed, preparing myself to

run out of the room, to confront Mom and Daddy. Then I remember that Mom had to go to the office, and Daddy's key chain with his bazillion keys wasn't in the key bowl when I came in.

Cole picks up the pieces of the picture and turns to place them on my bed. "Here, you can have it."

"Why? Why are they splitting up? Why like this?" This *cannot* be about the boutique. Daddy would never take his issues with Mom's work this far. None of their arguments ever get this serious. Not to say that the residue of black-blue words hasn't hung around for a few days here and there—house cold and quiet. But eventually someone cracks a joke or cuddles up or cranks up some nineties R&B or breaks out Monopoly or burps really loud, and things go back to normal. It's like they've always known the limit of how far they could stress their love. But this is way over the limit.

"He wouldn't say."

"He didn't say anything about why? Like, nothing?"

"You know there's no getting real talk out of Dad. I'm surprised I got that much," Cole says, picking up a couple of the photos around him.

"Well, did they get in a fight this morning after I left?"

He grabs another photo. "No."

"Did you see anything weird between them?"

"Not really."

"Come on, Cole! Something had to have happened!" I yell.

He lets out a long, hard sigh and then shifts his tired, swollen face into a bright smile. It's almost scary. "It was a normal Saturday. Mom went to work before I got up. Then Dad drove me up to the school for my tournament."

He's speaking in a high-pitched tone with a slow cadence, like he's reading a fairy tale to a bunch of first graders. This boy is not my brother. My brother is never this rude. I want to tell whoever this boy is to kiss my ass, but I don't because I need to hear what happened.

"He seemed cool in the car. Talked about the strengths and weaknesses of a few forwards from other teams and how he wanted to see a better follow-through from me. He left after the first game. He usually stays, but I didn't think anything of it. Then he picked me up and filled me in on what was going on with you. Didn't say two words on the way to the hospital, but you know how Dad's always lost in his head.

"Is that enough for you? Or do you want me to remember what we were listening to on the radio or how many red lights we stopped at or exactly where we were when the clock struck six or which way the wind was blowing when we drove under the live oaks on Rice Boulevard? Or maybe you want to know how many times Dad cleared his throat or scratched his chin. Because I can try to recall all of that if you need me to," he says, face still fake with cheer.

The sting of how ridiculous he just made me sound won't let me respond. *Am I really that stupid for trying to keep an eye out for things that might clue me in on my future?* I can't even approach the answer. The question has only been here two seconds and it's already changed my shape. And now it's like I don't fit right inside of myself.

"Sorry, I'm just tired," Cole says. He stands, picking up the rest of the photos and putting them back in his black storage boxes. "Give me a second and I'll be out of your room."

What? He dumps me in this foreign place, turns me into this foreign shape, and now he wants to leave me? *No!* I grab his hand.

He looks over at me in surprise.

The thing is, I'm usually the one trying to kick Cole out of my room. He's *always* in here. Says he likes staring at my walls. At the sketches and writings torn from my notebooks, at the images I'm drawn to in magazines . . . the photos he lets me keep . . . my favorite pieces from art classes over the years . . . all the poems and notes and lists and cards and quotes and random facts I collect. I've always figured that if I'm constantly looking at things that call out to me, then the Universe would eventually *have* to tell me what I'm supposed to do with my life. But it hasn't happened yet.

Cole squeezes my hand, lets it go, and gets back to collecting his photos.

"And what? Daddy told you to pass all this information along to me?" I ask, trying to slow him down. It pisses me off that Daddy would tell him and not me.

He grabs a black box off a stack of magazines on my desk. "No, he probably thought Mom would tell you," he says, and slides three photos behind a tab in the box.

"Mom didn't say anything to me. We talked about—" I almost tell on myself, but don't. On the way to get my car, I talked to Mom about the gallbladder attack finally being *the* sign to quit basketball. She's the only one who knows I want to quit. Known since I was in seventh grade and told her that getting my period was a sign to quit. Known I've been afraid to quit because I don't have a better dream to replace it with.

Daddy would die if he knew the truth. He's had a

basketball in my hands since before I could walk. If Cole knew, he would die, too. He *loves* basketball. And we've been playing each other our whole lives . . . pushing each other . . . supporting each other . . . defending each other when Daddy's too hard on us. Sometimes I wonder if we'd be so close if I didn't play.

Cole hasn't even noticed I stopped mid-sentence. It's like he's in a trance, focused on picking up and organizing his photos. "Oh, and we have until March eighteenth. That's the date we'll have to sit down with the judge and state which parent we want to live with," he says. I swear it's like someone has steamrolled over his emotions. Flattened him right out.

"That's not even six weeks! What if we refuse?"

"Then they'll have to spend a whole lot of time and money fighting over us. Believe me, I've already asked Dad these questions. And a million more. We need to choose. And I think we should stay together. It's one thing for Mom and Dad to get a divorce, but it's a whole different thing to split from you, too."

There's my brother. There's my Cole. "Me, too," I say, feeling the agreement soothe the hurt a little.

"Right now, I'm thinking we should stay with Mom. I don't like the idea of her being in the house by herself at night. Plus, we wouldn't have to go through the trouble of switching schools."

What about Daddy? I think. *What about the way his eyes go sad when he's alone? The way he can look scared even when he's sitting on a barstool eating pancakes.* "But you know Daddy needs us around," I say. "Mom will be fine. She's always fine."

Cole stops stacking his black boxes of photos and looks at me. "Do you really want to switch schools?"

"No." I feel lost enough as it is. I couldn't imagine throwing the change of a new school into the mix. *But still . . . Daddy.*

I stand up and grab the photo box at my feet. "Look, I'm not arguing in favor of Daddy or anything." *In favor.* The words taste greasy and bitter in my mouth. I hate them. I hate everything about this situation.

"I'm tired and I stink. Can we talk about this later?" Cole asks, and stacks another box.

"Okay," I say, walking over to him. I place the last box on top of the six others. And before he reaches down to grab them, I reach out for a hug.

He hugs me longer than I usually let him. And when he tries to let go, I hold on to him and hide my face in the ripe funk of his basketball clothes, where I feel safe. Where I'm just a sister. Not the girl whose parents are suddenly splitting up. Not the girl who has to choose which one to live with. Not the girl who's thinking about quitting the team, throwing all of her scholarship opportunities away, giving up everything she's worked for her whole life, and having the whole team, her daddy, and her brother probably hate her for it. And for what? The girl doesn't have a clue what to do with her life. Not a single fucking clue. I'm not ready to be alone with this girl.

I'm not ready.

I'm not ready.

I'm not ready.

Tears flood my face and I'm a 100 percent sure the ill-fitting girl inside me is going to explode.

"Everything will be okay," Cole reassures me.

He says it three times, and I still don't believe him.

REX

The house is freezing when I get home. My father must be here. With this house being so big and him being such a reclusive neat freak, the temperature of the house is one of the only ways I can tell the man is in. I never see his car because he keeps it parked in the garage, which is too small for my pickup truck.

My phone rings and it's Nya.

"Hello," I answer, and sit down on the concrete bench in the mudroom.

"Hey, heard about the game. Sorry you lost," she says.

"Thanks," I reply, and take off my LeBrons. The cold stone floor shocks the bottoms of my feet, even through thick socks.

"Heard you still had thirty-six points, though."

Did I? I think. Carli made me forget all about my stats.

"It never feels good losing, but at least that's a positive," she says.

Nya's big on positives. I like that about her. "True," I say, and store my shoes in a cubicle beneath the bench.

"So, did Danny have an off night?"

"Nah, not really."

"Oh, Jason was ball hogging again?"

"No."

"Well, what happened, then?"

I usually like that Nya asks a lot of questions. Keeps the conversation flowing, which I'll admit, I'm not always the best at. But tonight, the only answer to her questions is Carli. How do I tell her that?

"Oh, well. Can't win 'em all," she says, letting me off the hook. "I figured since y'all lost, you wouldn't feel like going to the movies."

But I can tell by the hope in her voice that she still wants to go. Hope that's making me feel terrible because I'm wondering what it would be like to take Carli to the movies. What it would be like to see her again. I have to see her again. "Yeah, it's probably too late now."

"Well, there's actually a midnight showing if you want to make that?"

"Sorry, I'm too tired," I lie, and make my way to the kitchen. When I get there, I open the fridge. "Arepas! Angie must've come today."

"A-what-who?"

I take the Pyrex out of the fridge and put it on the counter. "Let me tell you, Angie's arepas go so hard."

"Who's Angie?" Nya asks with a hint of she-bet'-not-be-a-side-piece in her voice, which doesn't even make sense.

I've already told her that I don't have time to waste trying to keep up with multiple girls. And even if I did, what kind of fool would I be telling her about one of them? "My babysitter," I say, and get a plate out of the cabinet.

"Babysitter?" Now she sounds confused.

I start preparing a plate of Angie's arepas and rosemary chicken (also bomb). "Well, she was my babysitter growing up." Damn, I miss Angie. She was the only person I had to talk to around the house. She started looking after me when I was born and my father decided to become a heart surgeon. He took forever. Twelve years, to be exact. Twelve years of never being home and studying in his room whenever he *was* home. Finally finished his residency two years ago, but nothing's changed. He's still always gone or in his room. Only difference is that now we live in this big-ass house in the boonies and I have a team that hates me. I pop the plate in the microwave.

"Oh," she sighs. "So she still comes by sometimes to make . . . wait, what's it called?"

"Arepas. They're these little corn pancake things filled with cheese," I answer, thinking about how Angie used to come over every morning and make them for me. That is, until she had a kid of her own. I was about nine.

After that she'd come over two or three times a week to bring groceries, make meals, and take me to games. Man, I used to get so hyped the days I'd step off the bus and see her blue Corolla parked outside our house. Having her around lifted me out of my father's cold silence.

But there's no escaping it these days. Now that we live way out here in Woodside, I can drive, and Angie has three kids; she makes it when she can, which is usually once a month. And that's if I'm lucky.

"They sound good. Maybe when you finally let me come over, I can try some."

"Shi—oooot," I say, catching myself, "these are as good as gone."

"I heard that," Nya says in a stern-mama type tone. See, she has this thing with cursing. Probably comes from going to church every Sunday. She's always inviting me, but I like to spend my Sundays outside, taking in the glory of trees and sky. Anyway, every time I curse, I owe her a kiss (with tongue) in the hallway beside her locker at school.

"But I didn't curse, though."

"Yeah, whatever."

"I didn't!"

"You almost did."

"Almost doesn't count," I say. I mean it's cool that I've had someone to walk the halls with the last few months, but I'm still not down with all that PDA stuff. I take out the apple juice and drink it straight from the jar. The sweet, cold liquid feels good running down my throat.

"What are you drinking?"

"Juice," I answer, and pour myself a tall glass—straight up liquid gold.

"So first you want to curse, and now you're over there sippin' on gin and juice?"

I chuckle. It's almost funny. I like how Nya can almost be funny sometimes. But I shouldn't be laughing at all. Not when I have to tell her about Carli.

The microwave beeps, but I don't get my food out.

"I have something I need to tell you," I say.

"What?" she asks.

I don't know why this feels so hard. I mean, what sixteen-year-old hasn't left one person for another person or told someone *I can't do this anymore* or straight up ignored someone until they stopped calling.

But Nya is the closest thing I've had to a friend since I've moved out here. Because I'm kind of quiet and mostly keep to myself, people are always making up stuff about me. Me being an arrogant asshole is my new team's favorite.

The thing that people don't understand is that when you spend a lot of time by yourself, you get used to keeping how you feel and what you think on the inside. But most people aren't having that. They need words. Words to put them at ease. Words to validate them. Words to excite and entertain them. And when you're not coming with the words they need, they'll start trying to figure out what's wrong with you. And when they can't figure it out, they have no problem making stuff up.

Learned that early, when the kids in my hood started calling me Half-taco. They said I didn't talk (barely said anything back then) because I could only speak Mexican. Used to piss me off so bad. First of all, Mexican is not a language. Second of all, Angie was Colombian and spoke better English than Spanish. If they wanted to be racist, they could've at least gotten their facts straight. But no.

So I'd fight. And when I got tired of that, I'd keep to myself. Had to walk a mile and a half to the basketball court at Emancipation Park, where all anyone cared about was ball, just to have some normal interaction with people. And by the time I was old enough to play ball for the school, I was used to keeping to myself. Used to being the dude everybody saw but nobody really knew. It felt safer that way.

I mean, the last couple years got better. Years and years of balling with the same people, and they start to get to know you a little. But then I moved out to Woodside.

The point is, I feel safe with Nya, less lonely with Nya.

And it's hard to give that up. But Carli. Carli makes me feel . . . everything.

"Well?" Nya says, sounding frustrated.

And it's the kind of everything that's not going away.

"Hello! Earth to Rex! What is it that you gotta tell me?"

I take a deep breath and push out, "I met somebody else."

"Who?"

The question comes at me with lightning speed. I want to say, *This girl you don't know* to keep things vague, but the ache in my throat won't let me call Carli something so impersonal. "Carli."

"Carli?"

I can hear her face twisting up.

"Who's Carli?"

"You don't know her."

"Did you have sex with her?"

"Whoa! Hold up a second," I reply, trying to think of why she would ask that. I didn't even think sex was on her brain. We never even got past touching above the waist with our clothes on.

"Well, did you?"

"No."

"Did you kiss her?"

"No."

"How long have you been talking to her?"

"I haven't been talking to her. I—"

"Well, when did you meet her then?"

"Tonight."

"At the game?"

"Yeah."

"Wait, is it that girl from the video?"

"You saw that?"

"Of course I saw it. Everybody saw it. So, is it?"

"Yeah."

"So, what exactly happened?"

"I caught her and—"

"So you already knew her?"

"No."

"Sooooo . . . you caught her and what?"

"I felt something."

"You felt something?"

"Yeah."

"Felt what?"

"I don't know . . . something deep."

She cracks up laughing in a way I've never heard her laugh before—hard and high, like she has her head thrown all the way back. "You felt something deep? That's the stupidest shit I've ever heard. And for a girl you don't even know? Everybody said you were an asshole, but I didn't know I was dealing with a fool, too."

My ear throbs with that familiar word—*asshole*—with the unfamiliar brand-newness of Nya. It's like she just smacked me upside the head through the phone. This can't be Nya. I wish I could clap back and call her a fraud, but shock has dulled my anger.

"But what can I say? You are *the* Rex Carrington. At least I got to try you out for myself. If you would've waited another two weeks, I would've given you the goods. But too bad for you, boo-boo."

No anger at my back, a fresh wound starts to spread just beneath my skin. I push it down to the place with the million other hurts I don't have time to deal with and hang up. Then I grab my juice, my plate out of the microwave, and sit at the counter on one of our uncomfortable-ass barstools.

Every time I have to sit on one of these, it pisses me off. Who buys concrete chairs? I would sit at the table, but those chairs aren't any better. All the furniture in this house is uncomfortable. My father says it has to match the house's modern style. Man, he can get on somewhere with his modern style.

Our old tiny house, with all of its worn upholstered furniture and wallpapered rooms and halls, where Mom had once walked and ate and slept and talked and been . . . where she'd been . . . was perfect if you ask me. But my father didn't ask me. He sold the house without—you know what, I'm not *even* about to start.

After a couple of bites, I look over at the opening to the hall that leads to my father's room. One look, that's all I'll allow myself. Sometimes, after I've been out here a while, he'll come out of his room and ask me about the game. And I'll ask him about the hearts he looked at that day and if he had a surgery. And we'll actually have something that resembles a conversation.

Okay, one more look, but that's it. The entry to the hall looks like an empty picture frame. The frame is modern (of course) with a wide, dark wood trim. And inside the frame, there's a white wall, illuminated by a small recessed light. Doesn't look like the frame is getting a picture tonight.

I eat my last bit of arepa, wash it down with juice, and carry my dishes to the sink. But before I rinse my dishes and put them in the dishwasher, I lean back against the counter and look at more pictures of Carli on her brother's IG feed. Her gentle face is the perfect antidote to tonight's roughness.

I have to give big ups to her little brother. Carli's social media is on lockdown, but Cole's is wide open. And he's a sharer, a big-time sharer. A big-time lover, too. Seems like every few weeks, a new girl takes over his feed. Not completely, though. Carli constantly gets play.

But tonight, Cole's posted a bazillion pics of their whole family together. Old vacation and family outing photos . . . things like that. And it's not even throwback Thursday. The gallbladder thing with Carli must really have him thinking about how much he loves his family. How perfect they are. What I would give to know that feeling for even one second.

After finishing my dishes, I head upstairs to my room. But before I reach the landing in the middle of the stairs, where my father's frame disappears from my line of vision, I turn around and look one more time.

Two minutes later I'm still standing here, staring at nothing.

This is stupid. I'll go knock on his door. If he doesn't answer, he doesn't answer. Wouldn't be the first time.

I walk back down the stairs and then down the hall that leads to his room. There's a slit of light underneath his door, and when I get closer I hear the faint sound of the TV. My knuckles are about to hit the door when I stop and think about how much he hates me.

The thing about it is, I don't blame him for hating me. I don't blame him for never wanting to be around me or talk to me. I get it. If I had never been conceived, Mom would still be alive. It's my fault she's not here. I've always gotten it.

But right now I need to share Carli with someone who won't laugh. Even though we have no history of talking about girls, and I'm pretty sure the conversation will be awkward as hell, I want to sit on my father's bed, like one of his patients, and talk about what I feel in my heart.

The slit underneath his door turns black, and the TV silences.

I lower my fist. It's all good. I'll go out back, lie under the trees, and talk to Mom, like I always do.

CARLI

I'm sitting in the gym after school on Wednesday, half reading a magazine and half watching my team run through plays. Even though I can't practice, Coach Hill still wants me here because I'm the captain, the leader of the team. I swear every time she reminds me of that, which is every chance she gets, an alarm goes off in my head. An alarm that's been sounding since Saturday. A reminder to tell her and the team that I don't want to play anymore. That I'm not coming back to play after the surgery tomorrow.

With my Spanish book open to hide my magazine tucked inside, I'm reading an article about how numbers can provide clues to your life's direction. The girl in the picture beside the article looks crazy-confident, like she knows exactly where her life is headed, and I'm trying to get a little bit of that.

Coach Hill blows her whistle, long and hard.

"Carli, watch out!" a few of my teammates shout.

I look up in time to miss a ball flying toward my head. It bangs loudly against the bleachers behind me.

"My bad," Vanessa, my backup, says with a way-too-sorry look on her face. I didn't see what happened, but I'm guessing she missed another one of Jordan's hard passes. It's really not her fault, though. Coach Hill plays me so much that Vanessa hardly ever touches the court. And now, with the playoffs so close, everyone's putting on the pressure for her to step up.

"Why don't you go ahead and take her out for the rest of the season?" Jordan, our point guard, yells at Vanessa.

The bestie can be a little overprotective. She's standing with her hands interlaced on top of her head—deep dimples in her milky brown cheeks even when she's mad.

If you only knew, I think before saying, "I'm fine," and get up to get the ball.

"Well, hurry up, then," Jordan says, and jokingly gives me the middle finger.

I smile, happy she's playing with me. We've been kind of distant this week. She's been complaining that I've been too quiet, that I've been keeping something from her. But there's no way I can tell her about quitting the team. And I can't tell her about my parents, either. Telling her would make it too real.

At least we've had Rex to talk about. She's convinced the kiss was at least partially for me. You see, he broke up with his girl hours after catching me.

Jordan knows because she has a cousin who has a best friend who has a boyfriend who plays basketball for Woodside who said that Rex broke up with his girl on the bus and everyone heard. Said she cursed Rex out so bad for leaving her that he had to hold his phone out of the window so he wouldn't have to listen to it all. Sounds crazy, I know. Why not just hang up in her face? Maybe because he's too sweet.

As I walk to get the ball, which bounced two rows down and rolled to the opposite side of the bleachers where the band always sits, I reach to touch the hospital menu in my back pocket, to make sure it's still there. I've been secretly carrying it everywhere with me since Saturday. Gonna write my number on the back and give it to Jordan to give it to Rex when he plays at our school Monday. I don't even have to tell you how bad I wish I could go (holding-my-pee-until-the-end-of-the-movie bad). But I'll be at home recovering from surgery.

After I retrieve the ball, I overhead pass it back to Jordan as hard as I can.

Jordan catches the ball and immediately drives down the lane for a layup, her tongue hanging out of the side of her mouth and the wristband on her left arm pulled up over her elbow.

"You ain't Michael!" I jokingly shout.

She makes the layup. "Oh, I'm not?" she asks, and walks the ball way out beyond the three-point line. She shoots and it drops.

"Oooooooo," the team says in unison. But I'm not even surprised.

Jordan has known since elementary school that she wanted to be the female version of Michael Jordan and has been pushing toward her dream ever since. I wonder if it has to do with her name.

I've been reading about this theory called normative determinism, which basically says that people's names can influence what they want to do with their lives. If Jordan is any indication, it's definitely true. Either way, I'm happy for her, I really am. But sometimes I get jealous that she has a dream and I don't.

"Okay, let's get back to work!" Coach shouts.

And back to the magazine. Here's what the article's telling me to do in order to get a clear look at my life's direction: write the numbers one to ten and beside them, list things that have happened the corresponding number of times this week.

Can't be trivial things, like how many Jelly Belly Buttered Popcorn candies I ate or how many times I've spotted Sabina Karlsson (this black model with red hair and freckles like me) in a magazine. Although I *have* been seeing her everywhere lately. They have to be things with meaning. Things with weight (with the way my life has been going, I should have no problem there).

And after I make the list, signs are supposed to start popping up with more frequency. Signs. Yeah, only the things I've been following since the fifth grade when one saved my life.

It was a Sunday. Daddy was getting ready to visit his parents' grave. I wanted to go, but he always insisted on going alone. So I went outside to practice my ball-handling skills in the driveway, hoping that when Daddy came out to get in his car, he'd be so pleased that he'd take me with him.

The basketball rolled into the street, and I ran after it without looking. Then a giant swallowtail, the largest butterfly in North America, swooped in. I'd cut one out of the *Houston Chronicle* after reading about its six-inch wingspan the day before. Tacked the photo up on my wall.

And there it was, in all its majesty, flying right in front of my face. I stopped suddenly, and a car whizzed by me so close that it felt like death giving me a cold hug.

And now, when the world is coming at me faster than ever—and I have to decide which parent to live with and how to tell my team I want to quit basketball and what to do with my life—I'm supposed to up and stop looking for signs just because Cole made me feel stupid? Exactly. So here goes:

1. Number of shoes Daddy removed before going to sleep on the sofa Saturday night after the hospital On Sunday I woke before

dawn and saw him asleep with his long legs hanging over the sofa's edge in the same clothes from the night before. I removed his other sneaker, covered him with a blanket, turned off SportsCenter, and went back to my room.

2. Number of Lucille Clifton poems I copied in my prettiest handwriting and placed on my wall while waiting to hear the kettle whistle from the kitchen on Sunday. Mom makes tea first thing every morning.

3. Number of words I said to Mom and Daddy when I walked into the living room I♭. It. True. Cole was still asleep. Mom looked confused. Initially, Daddy looked scared, like a little kid who'd just gotten in big trouble, but his lawyer side came through.

4. Number of sips Mom took of her tea as lawyer Daddy summarized the same details Cole had given me the night before. As usual, Mom tried to keep her cool. But her right pinky finger wasn't having it. It was tapping the hell out of her mug. Her right pinky was pissed.

5. Number of minutes that elapsed between the end of the conversation and Daddy

leaving to buy boxes from U-Haul

6. Number of exchanges Mom and Daddy had before Daddy moved out. All averaging ten seconds and all about which thing belonged to who.

7. Number of times per hour I begged Mom to tell me the reason they were splitting up.

8. Number of times this morning I thought I heard a knock at my door and got up and checked, but no one was there. Cole hasn't been in my room since Saturday night. Four days.

9. Number of times Daddy called me last night. The Rockets were playing the Clippers and he wanted me to study the rhythm of James Harden's step back. Normally I'd be annoyed, but every time I saw *Daddy* flash across my iPhone's screen, I was five years old again, hearing his keys jangling at the door, telling me he's home.

10. (x a thousand) Number of times I've closed my eyes and seen Rex's face. His big down-slanted eyes staring into mine. If only he could see my pain and come hold me now.

REX

When a mother tree is dying, she passes on messages of wisdom to her baby seedlings. No lie. Suzanne Simard, this badass forest ecologist, has actually traced messages moving down a dying mother's tree trunk, through the fungus in the ground, and into her seedlings. Dying trees speak to their children.

Crazy, right? That's my favorite thing to think about when I'm out here in the pine forest behind our house. Makes me think Mom spoke to me when she was dying, too. Makes me think, in the thirty seconds she held me on her chest before her heart stopped beating, she somehow gave me a lifetime of lessons.

I just wish I knew what they were.

TELL
ME

CARLI

Cole came into my room this morning *and* I get to see Daddy today. That's all.

REX

Yo! Once again my boy Cole comes through. He started to fall off for a minute. Hadn't posted all week. But this morning, on my way to school, he's making up for it—plenty! At the red light, I look down at my phone again and see he's posted another picture of Carli. She's riding in the backseat of their old-school Land Rover in a pink T-shirt with a rainbow. Underneath the rainbow the words *Easy Like Sunday Morning* are in gold, glittery letters. Man, easy is right. I swear it's never been easier to look at someone's face. And she's smiling so big. I mean huge.

They're on their way to Carli's surgery and Cole gave up *all* the deets. Say *what!* It's like he was personally giving them to me.

There's only one problem. Well, actually four.

1. I'd have to skip school and I have a precalc test second period. Dude, I studied all night for that thing. I *could* make it up next week, but a weekend is a long time to forget things like:

$$(a+b)^n = \sum_{k=0}^{n} \binom{n}{k} a^{n-k} b^k$$

2. I'd miss gym period, which is the mini-practice before tonight's game. I need that time to make my 111 shots a day. Gotta keep the jump shot dropping! Plus, Coach Bell will wonder where I am. I don't want to disappoint him again.

3. Carli's surgery will be at Houston Methodist in the Medical Center, the same hospital where

my father practices. Last time my father caught me skipping school (eighth grade, to try and stop this OG oak tree in the neighborhood from being chopped down by a builder), he didn't say a single word to me for weeks.

4. I hate hospitals. Haven't stepped foot in one since I was born. Every time I even drive by one, the world plops its fat ass right down on my chest, making it almost impossible to breathe.

But really, all these problems don't have shit on the promise of Carli. All week she's been glinting off the shiny parts still tucked inside of me. The pure and happy and hopeful parts, the parts starving for love. I'm telling you, it would kill me to miss this chance to see her. No question, all my shiny parts would go dull.

CARLI

When we get to the hospital, Daddy's already in the waiting room. He's sitting in a chair, hugging his briefcase, staring at the ground. Even though he's in his lawyer clothes, his scared little-boy face is in full effect.

See, this is exactly what I was trying to tell Cole. I hate seeing Daddy like this. Whenever I catch him this way, everything inside me plunges toward the place he must've gone when he was eight after hearing both of his parents died in a car accident. An endless pit with no sound or light.

I hope Daddy hasn't been sitting around his rental house like this. The thought of it makes me want to tell him that I chose him. Makes me want to tell him that I'm going to his place after surgery today.

When he sees us, he wipes himself clean of the little boy and stands up.

Without thinking, I run to him.

As I slam into his chest, he hugs me tight, lifting my feet off the floor. "Hey, Angel-face," he says.

"Hey, Daddy," I say, and as my feet touch the ground, my stomach growls super loud, like it's saying *Hi,* too.

"Hungry, huh?" Daddy says, and laughs. "Yeah, I remember when I tore my ACL in college and couldn't eat the night or morning before surgery. It was awful."

I've heard about his ACL a million times. Everybody has. He tore it mid-season of his senior year at Kentucky.

Left knee. Says it's what ruined his chances of going to the league. But right now I can hear about his ligament all day. Every word he speaks is filling up the massive hole his absence is digging inside me.

I want to tell him how strange it's been not having him home. How I've been missing his morning pancakes, the smell of his aftershave, the sight of his socks on barstools and sofas and tables, and his keys, especially his keys. But nothing comes out.

"Hey, Dad," Cole says, right behind me.

Dang, already? I feel like the girls on *The Bachelor* when someone interrupts their one-on-one time too soon. But I act like the bigger person and step aside.

Mom doesn't come into the waiting room. She's in the lobby, talking to the reception lady behind the large, circular desk. Mom must feel my eyes on her because she glances in my direction through her oversized shades before pointing toward a hallway. The reception lady nods, and Mom turns away and waves at us to follow her.

Walking down the hall, Mom's ahead with Cole and I'm lagging back with Daddy.

"How's the new place?" I ask Daddy, hoping it's full of those manila folders and flip-top boxes he's always bringing home from work. Better to be working than sitting around sad.

"It's nice. You'll have to come stay for a weekend as soon as you've healed up. I only signed a six-month lease because I plan to buy a house this summer, but I still want it to feel like home for you and Cole."

Way too much of the new reality rushes in at once, and I can't think of anything else to say.

Daddy ducks under a doorway. "You can do that thing you do to your walls, and I can help you transfer it all when we move. I've already helped you start. Hung a life-sized poster of Candace Parker in your room yesterday."

Astonishment helps me break my silence. "Really?" I say, but I want to be like, *Seriously, Daddy? Have you seen my walls?* Candace Parker can ball and all, but I don't have a single picture of a basketball player in my room. My walls are full of random things I love.

Maybe they haven't told me what I want to do with my life *yet*. But one thing's for certain: staring at a life-sized basketball player will tell me zero things about my future. I don't know how I'm going to take it down without hurting Daddy's feelings, but best believe it's coming down.

As I approach the elevator, Mom says, "The gastro-intestinal surgery department is on the sixteenth floor and you're sixteen!" Guess my feelings about that poster were still all over my face becase Mom only points out potential signs when she catches me with a sad or sideways look. It usually perks me up, but today it makes my mood worse.

You see, Mom doesn't believe in all my sign stuff. She's never said so, but she's not exactly big on believing in general. Well, believing in yourself, in your dreams, in love—those types of things—sure. But with everything else, she's always preached that questioning and studying is more important that believing. And every time she's asked me how my signs work, I've never had a good answer for her.

All I know is that I can't afford to miss them. What if the one time they clearly point me in the direction of what I'm meant to do with my life, I'm not even paying attention? What then?

I step onto the elevator, she pushes the circle with the sixteen, and it lights up. Sixteen years and the signs still haven't told me what I need to know most. I finally have the chance to quit basketball, but I still don't have a clue what to replace it with.

Mom's always telling me to be patient, to keep listening to myself and it will come. Yeah, easy for her to say. She's known she wanted to be an interior designer since she was a little girl, like Cole has known he wants to be a photographer or Jordan has known she wants to play basketball.

Sometimes I think about being a magazine editor, but then I think being a poet or writer would be cool, or maybe some type of visual artist, or a historian, or even an astrologist or a thrift shop owner. But I could also see myself as a professor. Or even an astronomer. It would be amazing studying stars, moons, planets . . . the whole universe. I don't know. At any given moment, I could have a million ideas about who I'm meant to be floating through my head. So what exactly am I supposed to be listening to?

Cole must see the angst on my face because he reaches for one of his hugs. I let him pull me in, and watch Daddy walk past us to the back corner of the elevator, as far away as he can get from Mom.

REX

I turn off the car. Check my phone again. Cole's posted a new pic of Carli walking into her hospital room with the caption "The strongest girl I know." She's looking back over her shoulder, scared.

"You're okay," I whisper, tracing the curve of her face with my finger. But her expression doesn't change.

My heart slumps and I'm out of my truck, hitting the lock button. I have a plan. I'm going to move as fast as I can. So fast I can't think about where I am.

Full-speed through the parking lot. I mean, my legs are moving so fast in these stiff jeans, I'm sweating. I swear February doesn't mean shit in Houston.

A minute later my red-and-black Air Jordan 1s hit the curb to the hospital entrance (like what!), and I'm walking toward the doors. Almost there. So close that the sliding glass doors part for me.

Then *bam*! Here comes the world's fat ass—thirteen million billion billion pounds—trying to sit down on my chest.

I turn around, walk away from the doors, and slide my right hand down the back of my neck, trying to get rid of the weight. But this hospital is extra heavy. Air is ripping in and out of the very top of my lungs—in-and-out and in-and-out and in-and-out so fast it burns. Feels worse than the final minute of a game I've played all thirty-two minutes of, when I'm sure my lungs are about to say, *I'm done*.

Come on, Rex. Hands interlaced on the top of my head,

I place one foot in front of the other until I make a wide circle around the porte cochère. Two wide circles and I'm breathing a little easier.

Turning back toward the doors, I nearly bump into a tall, brown-skinned man wearing a white coat over scrubs. My insides jump. He looks about ten years younger than my father, though. False alarm.

Back to the plan. *Let's go!*

This time I run (damn near fly!) through the doors and down the waxy hospital floors toward the elevators. Shoes squeaking, I pass a man walking in Wranglers and a cowboy hat like he's standing still.

In the elevator I close my eyes and see Carli's face in front of 1604. I push sixteen and it lights up. I can't believe I'm about to see her again. A mixture of ease and excitement wash over me. Then the metal doors slide closed, and I'm staring at my reflection.

My chest tightens.

I swear anytime I catch my reflection, it's looking at me funny. Thick brows (like my father's) tense like they wish I *would* step to them. Big lips (like my father's) perfectly still like they have nothing to say to me and never will. All my moles like tiny unforgiveable sins.

See, this is exactly why I don't keep a mirror in my

bathroom. Instead I keep a sticky note that says *You're good.* The only time I intentionally look in the mirror is once a week in the chair at the barbershop. Gotta make sure the high-top fade is on point.

And it is. Sponged the top this morning. Don't need to do much else but let the barber keep the lineup fresh. And I went yesterday, so I'm cool. With my fingertips, I brush the edge where my hair meets my forehead and tell myself, *You're good.*

But my reflection tells me that's a lie. *Dude, what are you doing? I don't remember anybody inviting you.*

And he's right. The only reason I know about Carli's surgery is because I've been stalking her brother's IG. What if she thinks I'm crazy when I show up? The red number above the elevator doors blinks to eleven, and I push buttons twelve through fifteen to buy more time.

When the doors open on twelve, two buff-looking dudes in blue scrubs walk on. "Thirteen plea—" the blond one starts before he sees it's already lit up. The dark-haired one stands behind him, talking about a lady over-waxing his eyebrows. Then a man rolling a pregnant lady in a wheelchair gets on and stands right beside me.

Really? I close my eyes and brace myself for the weight.

But it doesn't come.

We all start rising, and I actually feel the opposite of weight. It's the feeling I get sometimes when I'm sitting under the trees, when the wind is blowing just right and the sun is glinting down through the leaves. Like everything is okay. Like I'm right where I'm supposed to be.

CARLI

In the pre-op room, when I get Mom alone (Cole and Dad went to get a snack from the vending machine. Yes, they actually announced it in front of me like I'm not lying here starving), I try to take my mind off the surgery by asking her the same question for the millionth time:

What happened between you and Dad?

She's sitting beside me in a puke-pink pleather chair. Her sunglasses are off, and her eyes are definitely looking better than they did this morning. They've been in a perpetual state of red puffiness since last Saturday, but first thing in the morning, they're always the worst.

"I'll be fine," she says, looking up from a design budget. I guess she felt me eyeing her. She's had *I'll be fine* on repeat all week, mostly for Cole. She doesn't need to say it to me. I believe her. Mom always finds her way back to happy.

Found her way back after her first design business failed and she had to close her studio and start working from home again. We were in elementary school. Found her way back after her mom died from breast cancer four years ago. Grandma Rosemary was cool.

And it's not that fake, always smiling kind of happy. With Mom, it's like no matter what happens, big or small, she finds her way back to enjoying her work, her family (well, that's obviously complicated right now), her music, her books, her art, her random dance sessions, her tea, her candles, her long baths, her wine, her million trinkets around the house—her life. It's a kind of enjoyment that gets all up in your face, but in a good way. I swear if she didn't enjoy her life so damn much, I'd probably still be planning to ball. But I see her happiness and want it for myself.

"I know," I say, voice cracking. *Wait, where did that come from?* I'm not worried about Mom. I'm really not. But she has been crying a lot. The most I've seen since her mom died.

"Carli," Mom says, and puts her paperwork down. She has a look of concern in her big, Diana Ross–looking eyes. "Sometimes life hits you with things, but you have to keep going, you know."

Wait, what? I see what she's doing. She's trying to flip this conversation from her sadness to mine. But you know what, if she wants to do that, I'm going to use it. I reach down (don't have to reach very far) and pull out the sadness I've been feeling all week—about our family, Daddy, this whole situation—and I say, "It would help if I knew what happened." Tears pool at the base of my throat, and I gently guide them up behind my eyes and let them fall.

"Carli," Mom says, and picks up the Styrofoam cup from the nightstand. She takes a sip. There's a Lipton tea tag hanging by a string on the outside of the cup. Mom is bougie about her tea. No way she's enjoying that Lipton. "You want me to get you some ice chips?" she asks.

"Are you serious? I cry and all you offer me are ice chips?" I sit up in the bed and feel the chill from the cold room hit my bare back through the sparse ties of the hospital gown. "Forget ice chips! I want to know what happened between you and Daddy," I say, tears gone. Pretending gone. Patience gone.

I swear all fifty-two million times I've asked her about why she and Daddy are getting divorced, she acts shady, which is not like her at all. She never shies away from the truth. It's one of my favorite things about her. My whole life, I've always been able to ask her about anything. And I mean *anything*—sex, drama at school, drugs, alcohol, religion, masturbation. Yes, masturbation! But she can't talk about what happened between her and Daddy? Makes no freaking sense.

"You'll have to ask your dad, Carli."

"Seriously?" It's so irritating the way she keeps suggesting this like it's possible. I mean, I can ask Daddy about impersonal stuff, like how to craft the best arguments for my teachers to give me extra credit for all the random things I read. Or what I should use to get all my hair out of the drain. Or why we don't have one-person-one-vote if we live in a democracy.

But whenever I try to talk to Daddy about life outside the very practical or intellectual—basically anything dealing with feelings—he always gets that look in his eyes, that look that makes me stop pressing. After twenty years together, she might be immune to the look, but I'm not.

"Well, I can't talk about it, Carli. I wish I could, but I can't."

"You're the one always talking about questioning everything! And now I'm asking something that you have all the answers to, but you refuse to give them to me?"

"Look, Carli," she says. "I wish I could. I really do. But your dad has to be ready to talk to you about it, you know, or it won't do you any good."

"I'll take my chances."

"No, Carli."

"Seriously, if it doesn't do me any good, it'll be on me. I asked for it."

"I said no."

Cole and Daddy walk back in before I can get an answer out of Mom.

Dr. Williams is with them. "It's time," she says, two nurses right behind her. One comes over and releases the brakes on my bed, and the two of them together begin to steer me out of the room. Daddy, Mom, and Cole are right behind them.

I guess this is it. It all seems to be happening so fast. The nurses are wheeling me to a room where the doctors are about to take out a part of me . . . a part I've lived with my whole life . . . a part I might miss. What if I never wake up?

My bed clears the room and I'm moving down the hall, staring up at harsh, fluorescent lights.

When we come to a set of double doors, Dr. Williams presses a large red button on the wall, they swing open, and we all pass through, Daddy ducking. "The waiting room is just up there to the left," Dr. Williams says, and points to a space ahead with more puke-pink chairs arranged in a square.

The nurses turn me toward a long hall with more double doors.

Let my family come with me! I want to beg.

Cole grabs my hand.

"We'll be close, Angel-face," Daddy says, standing on my right.

Mom puts her hand on my left leg and says, "Just down the hall."

I look up at my family, all together, wanting so much I can't have. Wanting to wail like a baby, but instead I close my eyes.

REX

I make it just in time to catch Carli in the hall upstairs. When I see her, my heart starts floating in my chest. At least that's how it feels. Like there's nothing attached to it, like it might just go overboard and decide to float off somewhere. And that's without even seeing her face. Through the large glass windows on the double doors in the hallway, all I can see is her big red hair peeking up over the back of the hospital bed.

On one side of her, a beautiful tall woman with short natural hair is patting her leg. Must be her mom. And on her other side, her brother is holding her hand. Her dad (clearly where Cole and Carli get most of their height from) reaches down to give her a kiss on the forehead. Damn, she's lucky! Makes me want to push the red button and rush through the doors so I can join in on the love, too.

The nurses start to wheel Carli off, and I see her face. Hold up, she's scared. Her eyes are wide open, and her small, round nostrils are flared. Carli pushes up onto her elbow and turns back to look at her family. But walking away, her dad is looking down, her mom is gazing out a window, and Cole is busy with his phone.

Two fat tears fall down Carli's cheeks, and I'm sick. I hate seeing her like this. I wish I could rush in and hold her hand . . . rush in and tell her everything will be okay.

I press my forehead to the window of the door and mouth:

You're okay.
You're okay.
You're okay.

Over and over again. And before the nurses wheel her out of view, our eyes meet, her face rearranges itself to resemble something like peace, and I feel like I'm back in the gym, catching her again.

VERY
IMPORTANT
THINGS

CARLI

It's four thirty p.m. on Monday. Cole's at his game. Mom's back at work after taking the weekend off. And I'm sitting on the orange velvet sofa in the living room with my legs stretched out. I'm alternating between cutting very important things out of magazines and staring at a blank page in my notebook.

No more boys in my notebooks.

And definitely no more boys on my walls.

Instituted those rules after I kissed my first boy (Patrick) behind the bathroom stalls at basketball camp when I was twelve. After I got home, I must've written his name down in every color marker, crayon, and ink pen I owned. Then I waited for him to call, waited for him to ask me to be his girl, waited to put bursts of colors—bright, intoxicating colors—all over my walls.

None of it happened.

After Patrick, I might've been tempted to write a few more boys' names down, thinking they were true. But between side chicks, ego-tripping, dudes trying to get all big and bad, dudes thinking they could tell me what to wear or how to do my hair, dudes not doing what they said they would do, dudes being all sweet one second and not even texting me back the next, dudes trying to pressure me into sex, or dudes plain working my nerves, they were all false alarms.

But nothing about Rex feels false. I know this is going to sound crazy, but in the hospital, he came to me in a vision. There he was, on the other side of my operating room doors, same face drenched with the same tenderness.

It felt like déjà vu, as if it was the same moment I first saw him on the basketball court wrapped in different skin. Instead of burning up, I was freezing cold. Instead of catching me with his arms, he caught me with his words.

And now all I want to do is write down his name. And around and in between his name, I want to paste the things I just cut out of my magazine: a tree with blush-pink leaves, a luna moth with lime-green wings, a boy standing on a double helix reaching for purple stars. Signs I'm hoping will somehow find him in his dreams and let him know my heart.

But my rules.

Feel so small compared to what I feel for Rex. The smallest specks of dust in a gleaming stain-glassed cathedral.

I sit down in a pew, allow my long, skinny fingers to pull the royal blue Pigma pen from the crevice between open pages and write:

Rex Carrington

Rex Carrington

Rex Carrington

Rex Carrington

Rex Carrington

Rex Carrington

Rex Carrington

Over and over again until I'm beaming with a thousand colors. Then I scribble tiny hearts around his names in the shape of a giant heart. Does it look like the work of a first grader? Sure, but ask me if I care.

Outside, the yellow school bus stops in front of our house. Through the window above the sofa, I see Cole hop off.

"Let's go!" Cole shouts as soon as he's in the house. A few fast and squeaky footsteps across the wooden floor, and now he's standing in the entrance of the living room in his basketball warm-ups, out of breath. He's not supposed to be here. His game starts at five. His team is shooting around, like, right now.

"Go where?" I ask, alarmed, my mind sprinting off to the worst fear it can find. Car accident. Mom and Daddy. I quickly lift my legs and turn around so that my feet are on the ground. *Ouch!*

"Rex is playing at our school tonight, and I've decided that you're coming."

I let out a sigh. "You seriously came all the way home for that? What's wrong with you?" I yell. "You know I can't go anywhere."

"What's wrong with me? Really? I don't get you, Carli," he says, face going bright red like he's about to explode from exasperation. "You know . . . you're always worried about what this random thing means and what that completely arbitrary thing means. But when something simple is staring you right in the face, it's like you don't see it. I should be at my game, right now, but I'm standing here ready to take you to see Rex. And you're really telling me *no*?"

I want to get defensive, but the bright sun swinging inside my chest won't let me. I can't believe I've never considered going to the game. Maybe because my stomach hurts like hell. Or because the doctor ordered me to stay home until Wednesday. Or because a teacher or coach or any of my teammates could spot me. But they're even smaller than the smallest specks of dust—not *even* about to stop me from seeing Rex.

REX

Carli. Is. In. The. Building. Can you believe it? I mean, I dreamed of her coming, but there's no way I thought she'd be here this soon after surgery.

I'm sitting high up in the stands, a couple rows above my team. The JV game is about to start. Carli's walking along the sidelines with Cole, who's suited up for the game. A few of his teammates, standing in a huddle around their coach, look back at him like, *What the fuck?* But he doesn't pay them any mind. His attention is on Carli, his arm around her for support. And judging by how slow they're moving, she needs every bit of it.

I stand up, ready to run to her and relieve him so he can get on the court.

But the first horn on the game clock sounds, and I sit back down.

Coach is sitting in the bleachers above me, so he can keep a good eye on the team. He likes us to stay put during the JV games, stay focused. I mean, we can run to the bathroom or go get a bag of chips from the vending machines if we want, but if he catches anybody wandering around trying to holla at girls, he benches them for the game.

But man, this feeling inside me right now has me thinking crazy. Has me thinking this moment is bigger than a game on the bench. Has my whole body feeling like it's about to explode into some rainbows and shit. I'm telling you, another minute of trying to contain it, and people are gonna be picking me up as Lucky Charms scattered around the gym.

The second horn sounds. Game time. *Man, forget this.* I run down the bleachers and sidelines until I'm standing in front of Carli, looking straight into her brown eyes, taking in their surprise, their delight.

I wrap my arm around her other side. "I got her," I tell Cole, and he flashes me a giant smile before letting go.

CARLI

Rex's hand is around my hip and I'm floating. Dreaming. I must be dreaming. Sleepwalking. I must be about to fall flat on my face. But the strength of Rex's hand holding me up, the light grip of his fingers pushing into my skin, the tingles moving up and down my left side and through my body, tells me I'm not. Tells me this is real, just like I thought.

"Hi," he says, in a low voice, his smiling eyes wandering across my face.

"Hi," I say in return, and let my eyes travel, too. From the tight, spiraling curls in his high-top . . . to his thick brows . . . to his hooded eyes . . . to the mole on the right side of his nose . . . to his big, curvy lips. I can't help but pause there for a bit. They look so soft.

"Is here good?" he asks, and points to the opening on the first row we're standing in front of.

"Perfect," I say, thinking about how I'm going to get my butt all the way down to the wooden bench without ripping my stomach open. He must read my mind because as we turn to sit down, he pulls my body closer to his until he's taken almost all of my weight and our bodies are sitting down as one.

After we sit down, we hold hands, interlocking our

fingers. It's automatic. Like we've done it a million times.

My hand is on top—his long, brown fingers reaching over my knuckles showing his short, shiny nails. Not just-got-them-buffed shiny, more like really clean shiny.

Looking over my left shoulder, I take in more of him—the way his strong neck eases down into his collarbones, the way his chest bulges underneath his dark green uniform, the way he smells like a pine forest. It's making me want to lean in, put my nose right up to the crook of his neck, and take a sniff. Or maybe even kiss his chin or bite his cheek or eat him up or have him eat me up or bury myself forever inside his earthy-sweet-smelling uniform. Clearly, I'm losing my mind being this close to him.

● REX ●

My nervousness makes me start bursting with words, spitting them out right and left. "It's crazy you're here. Man, that surgery had to be no joke. How are you feeling? I can't believe you're actually here . . . sitting next to me. Sorry, you'll have to excuse me . . . it's just that I've been dreaming . . .

nah . . . never mind. You healing okay, though? Cole said you've been feeling better every day." This is not me. This is not how I talk. It's like some whack, diarrhea-of-the-mouth dude has invaded my body and won't shut up.

"Cole, my brother?" Carli asks, sparse eyebrows scrunched together.

Damn, I just told on myself, didn't I? Now how am I supposed to explain knowing her brother's name? I guess I could make up a different Cole. But what other Cole would know how she's been? Even if I *could* get my mouth to slow down and be cool long enough to formulate a lie, that one wouldn't even make sense.

She lets go of my hand and grabs a round, gold pendant hanging from her necklace. She slides it back and forth slowly along her chain, eyeing me curiously.

Sweat rolls from under my arm, down my side, and I unzip the jacket to my warm-ups. "Yeah, your brother," I say, pushing the words past the knot at the back of my throat screaming, *Don't mess this up!*

"You know him?" she says, looking confused—pale, bare lips clasped tight, every freckle sprinkled on and around her nose giving me the eye.

"No, I started following him on IG after you passed out a few weeks ago. Wait, it wasn't a few weeks. Feels like it, though. Feels like forever. When was it, again?"

"Saturday before last," she says, studying my face.

"Saturday before last, yeah . . . after you passed out,"
I repeat like a bumbling fool and look down, feeling my
face go long and soft. If Carli's still reading me, she can
definitely see how scared I am.

"So, you're basically telling me you've been stalking me
on my brother's Instagram?"

Shit. I will every muscle in my face to go stiff. Now she
probably thinks I'm pissed, but it's better than her seeing how
many hours I've spent staring at her face on the Internet. I
can't have her thinking I'm some type of weirdo. I can't lose
her like this. I swear I can't. Just thinking about it is making
my throat swell up, making my insides turn black.

My face accidentally slips into softness again, and I can
feel her eyes—a warm glow—looking around inside of me.

CARLI

Everything in me wants to kiss him. Not because his lips
look about as delicious as delicious gets (and they do!), but

because everything I've been feeling for him, I can see he's been feeling for me, too.

Plus, his nervousness is about the cutest, most kissable thing in the world. He'd better be glad I'm not selfish. If I was, I wouldn't even think about putting him at ease. "Kidding . . . kidding. You wanted to check on me?" I say, letting go of my necklace. "That's sweet."

He lets out a long sigh. "Yeah, I wanted to make sure you were okay," he says, looking up, his wide mouth cracking a small smile. But the rest of his face is still long, like it hasn't gotten over me playing around.

Dang, now I feel bad. I hope I didn't hurt him. "Trust me, if you had anything besides highlight clips on your Instagram, I would've been stalking you, too."

His face brightens way up. "Oh, you looked?"

A strange lightness rushes to the center of my forehead. I can't ever remember making a boy so happy. It feels so reassuring, so good. "Of course. Had to do my background research."

"Is that right?" he says, grinning, and tilts his head to the side. His nose is crooked, like maybe it's been broken a few times. I wish I could kiss that, too.

"Not that it gave up any goods on you. You don't have any real pics on there. No friends. No ex-girls. Nothing but basketball stuff. And nobody has time to be sitting around watching you dunk and drain threes all day," I say.

He smiles big, like I'm making his day.

But I'm greedy. I want to make his year, his life. So I gently reach for the menu in my back pocket. The one I wrote the fact about kisses on before I even knew how he felt about me. The one I carried around in my back pocket for over a week—steady stream of hope coming from my right butt cheek. Rex is about to flip when he sees it. But it's not there. "Damn," I mumble, remembering the menu is with Jordan and she's not coming until the end of Rex's game.

"Oh, is it your stomach?" Rex asks, thick eyebrows raised in concern.

"No, I'm okay."

"What is it then?"

"Nothing."

"You can tell me."

"Don't worry about it. I'll tell you later."

"Why can't you tell me now?" he says.

I'm a little surprised by his persistence, but it feels kinda nice. Like we've skipped right over the beginning phase of our relationship, when people hold back trying to say and do all the right things. Like we're already in this thing deep. "Because," I say.

"Because what?"

"*Because* it'll be better later," I explain. For the full effect, I want to give him the menu in person. Telling him about it wouldn't be the same.

"I hate when people do that."

"Do what?"

"Tell you there's a secret without telling you the secret."

"Secret? There is no secret," I say, now wondering if we're having our first argument.

"Yeah, you just told me there was something to tell and simultaneously told me you can't tell me what it is."

"No, I said *damn*, and then you got nosy."

"Well, if you weren't going to tell me, why not keep the *damn* to yourself?"

I could be cool and say, *It slipped out*, but I decide to push back and ask, "Why you gettin' mad?" He actually sounds more worked up than mad, but the question itself usually makes people mad, and I'm kind of curious what he'd be like mad.

Don't get me wrong, I'm not trying to start something for the sake of starting something, but he's already taken it this far. And if he's the type who grits his teeth or clenches his fists over stupid shit, the type I could see yelling and name-calling and trying to humiliate, the type who makes my insides either want to curl up into a tight ball or grow sharp teeth, I need to know now. Because no matter what the signs say or how many fuchsia flowers he has blooming in my chest, I'm not *even* about to deal with that.

But his face grows long and soft before he lowers his head again. When he got like this earlier, I thought it was nerves. But now I see it's something else . . . something deeper that hurts. And he's sitting up here showing it to me in a way no other boy has before.

The pain inside me peeks its head out, eyeing a friend. And now it's like his hurt and my pain are hiding under the bleachers together, holding hands.

 REX

I swear I hate myself. "Sorry, I didn't mean to," I say, and look up. Her pale face has blurred. A thin layer of tears coats my eyes. Lots of blinks, really fast, and it's better. But what does it matter? She's not gonna want me. She's already seen how messed up I am.

"Hey, it's okay," she says, and interlaces her long, soft fingers with mine.

"No, it's not!" I say, harder than I want to. *What the hell is wrong with me? Oh, yeah, this is the way to show Carli how I feel about her. I swear I'm so stupid. This is exactly why I usually keep my mouth shut.*

She looks down at her high-top burgundy Nike Blazers, but doesn't take her hand away from mine.

I slowly slide my thumb back and forth over hers, gently squeeze her hand, and rub my thumb back and forth again, hoping my hand will speak for me.

She briefly looks up at me but looks back down. My hand is not gonna cut it.

"Sorry, I'm not usually like this," I start to explain, but I stop because my eyes are glazing over again. *What the hell?* I swear it's like everything inside of me, everything I usually try to keep on lock, has up and decided it wants to come out and lay bare at Carli's feet. But can it hold up a second?

She looks back at my thumb, sliding back and forth over hers.

"I'm usually quiet," I start again. "But I don't know what's happening to me. It's like I don't know what to do with everything I'm feeling right now . . . where to put it all. And it's coming out in weird ways."

Her eyes meet mine, then start wandering around my face.

"Not to say, I don't get hype. I mean, when it comes to basketball, I'm like a different person. Or if somebody steps to me, now that's a whole different story. I mean, I let a lot of shit slide, but some shit—" *Damn, Rex. Go ahead and curse up a storm, why don't you.*

Her eyes return to mine, like she's waiting for what else I have to say.

"I'm just finding it really hard to act normal around you."

She bites the inside corner of her bottom lip, like she's thinking, but she doesn't say anything.

"But in a way, talking like this is making me feel more normal than I've ever felt," I continue, words pushing up and out of me like, *we got this.* I sure hope they know what they're doing. "It's weird being quiet all the time. Keeping everything inside. It's like nobody ever really gets to know me. I'm not gon' lie, letting it all out feels weird, too. So weird. Man, I feel crazy-exposed. But in a way, it feels good. I want you to know me, Carli. Like, straight up. And I'm really sorry for things coming out wrong earlier. It's just that this saying-how-I-feel thing is new to me. So new. Like, you don't even understand."

"I can't even imagine you being quiet," she says, her eyes searching me again.

"I know. It's weird," I say, happy she's not done with me yet.

"I see you like the word *weird.*"

"What do you mean?"

"You just said it, like, five times."

"Did I?"

"Yeah, back in the day-day-day it used to mean *destiny,* you know?"

"Really?"

"Yeah, it used to be spelled with a *y,* like *w-y-r-d,* but it got all messed up when Shakespeare— Wait, are you sure you want to hear about this?"

"Yeah."

"Don't say *yeah* just to be saying *yeah.* Because I don't want to be sitting up here wasting all my breath if you're really not that interested," she says, and reaches into the right pocket of her jean jacket with her free hand.

"I'm one hundred percent interested," I assure her. How could I not be? She's trying to teach me something I don't know.

She lets go of my hand. "Well, there were these three Weird Sisters, right," she explains, opening what looks like a tiny box of movie popcorn. She taps the box against her palm and three light-yellow jelly beans roll out. "Want some?"

"No, thanks," I say. I'm more of a chocolate person, but mostly I want her to get back to the story.

She pops the jelly beans into her mouth, closes the box, and puts it back in her pocket. "Wait, I guess for all of this to make sense, we have to take it back to Greek mythology. Okay, there were these three weaving goddesses called the Fates, right."

I nod.

"I forget their names, but one spun the thread of human fate, one gave it out, and one cut the thread, basically deciding when people died. Talk about girl power. Doesn't get more powerful than deciding people's destinies. Even their daddy Zeus couldn't tell them what to do," she says, smacking and then swallows.

"Anyway, the three sisters had that staying power, too. They kept going strong through Roman mythology, with name changes here and there, and then made it all the way to *Holinshed's Chronicles* as the Weird Sisters. Holinshed was ones of the guys in charge of writing this book about the UK's history back in the sixteenth century. Apparently Shakespeare, like a lot of writers of his day, was really into the *Chronicles* and used it a lot in his plays."

She pauses, shifts her bottom jaw to the right, and slides her tongue back and forth under her cheek. Must be some jelly bean stuck to her teeth. Don't ask me why but seeing her trying to get it out is making her look cuter than ever.

"Got it?" I ask, smiling.

"Yeah," she says, and looks down for a second, like she's embarrassed.

"Continue . . . continue."

"Okay, so where was I?"

"*Holinshed's Chronicles.* Shakespeare liked using it for his plays."

"That's right," she says, tilting her head back and to the side.

"Don't act surprised. I told you I was interested."

"All right, then," she says, smiling. "So, when Holinshed and his people wrote about the Weird Sisters, they described them as these beautiful nymphs and fairies, right? As these goddesses of destiny. But when Shakespeare wrote about the three sisters—well, remember the Weird Sisters in *Macbeth*?"

"No," I answer, feeling stupid. We just read that play in English last year, but I have no idea. And I thought I was smart. I mean, your boy *has* gotten straight As since the first grade. But Carli's more than good-grades smart. She's that nonrequired-reading kind of smart.

"No? Okay, well, they were these strange-looking witches with beards who foretold Macbeth was gonna murder that dude Duncan. Anyway, Shakespeare knew exactly what he was doing by making the sisters witches. At the time people were losing their minds over witchcraft. Blaming it for everything bad. So by turning the Weird Sisters into these strange witches, Shakespeare gave his play that extra hype. Got everybody all scared and fascinated and whatnot. And basically changed the word *weird* forever."

"Word?" I say, staring at Carli in amazement. "Why didn't I know that?"

"Well, it's not exactly like they teach it in school. But wouldn't it be cool if they did? Or at least if they gave some bonus points for knowing random things? It's crazy, it's like every school wants to teach everybody the same exact things, like those are the only important things in life to learn about. But there are sooooo many things in this world to know. Who decides what's most important, anyway? And why do they get to decide?"

CARLI

Usually when I run my mouth this long around a boy, I start feeling stupid, like I need to superglue my lips shut. But the way Rex is looking at me—eyes wide and glazed over with gleam, like he's staring at something sparkling—is making me feel like there's some kind of hidden jewel inside me.

"So, I'm taking it that you're the question-authority type," Rex says, reaching for my hand again.

I interlace my fingers with his. "Never really thought about it like that, but I guess my mom does always say to question everything."

"Your mom sounds cool."

A wave of irritation rushes up inside of me at the thought of Mom. At the fact that her eyes haven't been red and puffy for the last two days, and she seems to be getting back to normal (not that I wanted her to cry forever, but this fast?). At the fact that she still hasn't told me what happened between her and Daddy. "Yeah, but having so many questions leaves me with a lot of stuff unanswered."

"You mean Google doesn't have all the answers?"

"I wish!" I say, and laugh. Then I ask, "What's your sign?" I'm thinking he has to be an Aries. He has way too much honesty, even when he's trying to be funny, to be anything else.

"My sign?"

"Yeah, like, when were you born?"

"August second," he says, briefly looking down.

"Oh, a Leo. I can see that, too. Your passion. Not to mention how bold you are."

"Bold?"

"Well, you *did* come down here putting your arm around me like you knew me and thangs," I say with a playful attitude.

"Well, you *are* sitting here holding my hand like you know me and thangs," he mimics me in a high voice, then laughs low and deep.

"That's not how I talk," I say, cheesing, and bang my knee against his.

"I know," he says, his voice turning serious. "I'm not gonna lie, though. I *do* already feel like I know you. Not know-you-know-you, obviously, because I just met you. But it's like somehow, I've always known you. Like it took me seeing you to remember. Wait, that doesn't even make sense. It's hard to explain. It's like . . . man, I don't know."

"I know what you mean."

"You do?"

"Yeah," I say, "it's just this feeling."

"Exactly . . . this feeling," he says, sliding this thumb gently back and forth across my thumb. "And it didn't waste no time. I swear it started the first moment I saw you on the court."

"Same here. It's like I didn't even know what was happening to me. I literally thought you, or what I was feeling for you, was why my body was freaking out."

"No you didn't," he says, and laughs.

I laugh, too. "Yes I did! And then it was crazy because I had this . . . No, never mind."

"Had what?"

"I've been thinking about you a lot, that's all," I say, not wanting to spoil the vision of him. How real it felt.

"That's not what you were about to say."

No denying that, I look down. But the soft whirling in my chest makes me look back up. "I had a vision of you."

"Word?" he says, still sliding his strong thumb gently across my thumb. "What did you see?"

"Well, you were at the hospital that day I had surgery. It was crazy how real it felt."

His face lights up. With all seriousness, if the power in the gym were to go out right now, there would be a beam of light coming from right beside me. "It wasn't a vision. I was there," he says.

"What? But how?"

"Cole posted where the surgery was going to be that morning, and I had to go . . . had to see you. I don't usually do things like that. But you got me . . . man, I don't know. I've never felt like this before."

His words make me feel beyond good. It's like every cell in my body is twerking and cartwheeling and high-kicking all over the place. *I don't usually do things like this, either. . . .*

 **REX**

Carli is kissing me. And it's warm and soft and wet and sweet. Her lips sandwich my bottom lip and then my top . . . bottom, top, bottom, top, her tongue sliding over mine in between. A final press into both of my lips, and she pulls away far enough to look at me.

But the way her eyes are moving around my face feels like she's still kissing me. "One . . . two . . . three," she counts.

"Three what?" I ask, smiling, and reach up to touch her hair. A risk. Trust, even before Solange's song "Don't Touch My Hair," I received the memo. But Carli just kissed me, so I figure I get a pass. Plus, I've never seen hair so big and long and red and brown and kinky and coily on one person's head at the same time. It's soft and smells like jasmine.

"Four . . . five . . . six. Oh, that one's nice," she says, and turns to touch my face with her free hand. She grimaces and straightens out a little. "But I think I like this one best," she says, and rubs her pointer finger in a tiny circle on the side bridge of my nose before bringing her arm back down.

She must be talking about my moles. I hate my moles. Hardly ever have to see them since I avoid mirrors. But hearing her talk about them is almost making me want to break out my phone and look at myself. *Almost.* Instead, I bend down and press my lips to her hand. Then I lift her hand—slightly, gently—and hold it between my hands. "Thank you," I say.

"Sure thing," she says, and nods.

"No, not about the moles."

"So, what are you thanking me for then? Kissing you?" she asks, head cocked to the side, cute and confident as can be.

"No," I say, and laugh, trying to think of a good way to

put it. But I can't. Man, it's like one day I'm getting through life alone, hanging on to any kind of happiness I can find. I mean, I'm doing pretty good, despite the circumstances.

But then—*bam!*—here Carli comes, and it's like a whole new world. A world where I don't have to feel so damn lonely anymore. "A whole new wooorrld," I'm singing before I can even stop myself. Man, this girl has me acting corny as hell!

She laughs the cutest laugh, high-pitched and throaty, with her button nose pinching along the bridge and her straight white teeth showing.

I'll be a cornball all day every day if this is the reward.

"*Aladdin?* You are not singing the *Aladdin* song right now!"

And then a different voice, a much deeper voice, from behind, "Rex!"

A whistle blows. Sneakers squeak against the gym floor. People around us chant "Defense!" as our JV team takes the ball up the court. Two girls, a bench up behind Carli, are snickering and looking at us. Trying to reorient myself to the world outside of Carli is making me dizzy. Everything's rushing at me all at once.

"Rex!" I hear again, closer.

Carli looks up, over my right shoulder, and the residue of laughter wipes clean off her face.

CARLI

"Rex!" A short, muscly man walking up behind Rex shouts. He looks pissed, eyebrows pulled down over his small eyes. He needs to stop, lift those brows back up. His hairline-forehead combo is unfortunate enough. It's like they can't stand to be around each other—forehead jutting forward and hairline running back—far, far away.

Rex lets go of my hand and stands up.

The man walks past us and makes a strong wave motion for Rex to follow. The man is wearing khakis and a dark green vest over a white polo shirt, which is way too tight around his biceps. Dark green and white, same colors as Rex's warm-ups. That's got to be his coach.

Rex follows him to the side of the bleachers, near the entrance, where the man snatches Rex by the elbow. Rex doesn't pull away. Then with his other hand, the man starts waving his pointer finger in Rex's face.

Look, I get chastising players for not being where they're supposed to be . . . not sitting with the team. Coach Hill does it, too. Makes us run suicides the next day after school. But is all this finger-waving and elbow-grabbing business really necessary? This man is being extra.

And Rex is standing there taking it. He's more than a foot taller than the man, but by the way he's standing with his head all down and his shoulders all hunched over, you can barely tell. It's like he's leaning into the verbal beating. I hate it.

Doesn't Rex know who he is? He's Rex Carrington! He's ESPN's high school player of the year, for Christ's sake! And I wish I could remember all the other things Cole told me, but it's a lot. Way too much to be standing there taking that man's shit.

Rex wipes his face.

And then I realize he's crying.

And this familiar feeling shoots through me. It's the same deep-throated darkness I feel when I see Daddy sad. Everything in me wants to go to Rex. Wants to tell that man to fuck off. But I'd only get him into more trouble.

Head hanging, Rex exits the gym without looking back. When his coach walks past me, I catch him giving me a once-over.

Fifteen minutes later Rex comes back through the gym's double doors in street clothes—gray T, black Nike joggers, and some Jordans 1s. Damn, I can't believe his coach is benching him for the game. Because of me.

Along the sidelines Rex walks toward me but won't look at me. Won't even look in my direction.

My eyes are on his eyes, pleading with them to connect, but he looks straight ahead, gaze cold. Everything in me freezes with the fear that this thing between us that only just began is already over.

He's three strides away from me, and my eyes are practically on their knees begging him to look at me, but he won't even give me a glance. Two strides and still nothing. One stride, and all the color inside me starts to drain. He's passing me and it's over.

But when I hang my head, I see a small, folded note in my lap.

THE
SUM
COLOR

● REX ●

I'm sitting at my desk trying to figure out how many four-digit numbers there are with at least one repeating digit, but I can't even concentrate. It's almost midnight, and Carli still hasn't called.

What if she didn't get the paper with my number inside? My shot *has* been off lately. It could've missed her lap and landed on the floor. Or what if she got it and decided not to call? Man, I felt like such the asshole walking right past her and not saying anything. But I couldn't get into any more trouble.

I'm no closer to solving the problem when my phone rings. My heart leaps, but it's only Nya. She's been calling and texting with weak apologies since last Sunday—she didn't know what she was saying . . . it was the devil . . . please take her back. Straight to voice mail, where I've been sending her. She calls again. Straight to voice mail. And again. You already know.

Another five minutes and my phone rings with a number I don't recognize. It could be Nya calling from a friend's phone. Plenty of girls have gotten me with that trick. But what if it's Carli? I can't take the risk. "Hello," I answer.

"Hey, it's Carli."

"Hey," I say, relieved.

"Hope I'm not calling too late. Just got off the phone with my dad."

"It's all good. You gave me some more time to try to figure out this math problem for a little extra credit."

"Did you figure it out?"

"Nah."

"You want me to let you go?"

"Nah, never. I mean, nah. Just plain nah. Not *never*. *Never* would be weird." *Really, Rex?* I stand up, trying to rid myself of these damn nerves. I thought they'd gotten used to Carli at the gym, but a few hours of separation and they don't know how to act again.

"I swear your nervousness is the cutest thing ever,"

Carli says, and hits me with a little high-pitched laugh that calms me down a bit.

I walk over to my bed, pick up the three T-shirts that lost in the what-to-wear battle this morning, and toss them onto my desk chair. "I have all week to figure it out, though. Mrs. Johnson only gave us the problem today."

"Dang, you must love you some math."

"Yeah, it's cool," I say, and lay back on my bed. I want to tell her that it's mostly a means to an end. That one day, after basketball takes me however far it will take me, I want to be a landscape architect. I want to design dope spaces that will bring people closer to trees. And my math needs to be on point for that. But just thinking about saying so many words right now is making my nerves act up again.

"What's your favorite number?"

"I don't know. I guess if I could name the largest number at any given moment, that would be my favorite."

"Really? Why?"

"I don't know. There's something reassuring about the fact that numbers never run out . . . that they keep getting higher and higher, forever and ever. It's like numbers never really die."

"Oooo, I like that," she says, in a voice that takes my

mind back to kissing her. "But I thought you would've said twelve."

Her shadowy lips pull away from mine, and I'm back to staring at my white ceiling. "Yeah, I guess twelve is my lucky number. It was on the very first practice jersey I wore. Picked it out of a bag at my first basketball camp when I was seven, and I've kept it ever since."

"The number twelve is super connected to the cosmic bodies, you know."

"Oooo, I like that," I say, mimicking her again. Partly because it made her laugh when I did it earlier at the game, but mostly because it feels good having the sound of her in my mouth.

"Yeah? Well, I have more where that came from. Did you know that the moon moves twelve degrees around its orbit every day?"

"Nope."

"Well, it does. And you know there's twelve months in a year because they chopped up the number of days it takes the Earth to rotate around the sun by the number of days it takes the moon to rotate around the Earth, right?"

"Yeah, I think I knew that," I answer, although I'm pretty sure I didn't.

"And there are twelve zodiac signs."

"You're really into that kind of stuff, huh?"

"Yeah, *that* kind of stuff is interesting to me," she says defensively.

"Sorry, I didn't mean it like that. It does sound interesting," I try to assure her.

But she doesn't respond.

I bring my hand up to my forehead, trying to think back to what I said and how I said it and how it might have hurt her, but I can't find my crime. Doesn't matter, I'm clearly guilty. I want to apologize and tell her I didn't mean it, but I've already said that. Seconds of silence pass, and they feel like forever. "Sorry about earlier at the game. I would've stopped and said good-bye, but my coach."

"It's okay. I hope I didn't get you into too much trouble," she says, sounding like she's already forgiven me.

I relax my arm back down by my side.

"I can't believe your coach made you sit out the game. He seems like a real asshole."

Her criticism of Coach stings, but I say, "Nah, he's cool. Just trying to make sure I stay focused, that's all." I don't tell her that Coach comes up to the school every morning at five thirty a.m. to open the gym for me. I don't tell her that he's always studying my game so he can help pinpoint areas that need improvement. I definitely don't tell her that he believes in me. Or that his belief in me often makes me wish that I was his son.

Meanwhile, I haven't seen my real father since last week. I literally have not seen him or any evidence of him. The house hasn't even been cold. But telling her that my coaches have always been the closest thing I've had to a dad is out of the question.

"But he was all up in your face. I mean, was it that serious? Your game wasn't even close to starting."

I roll over on my side and stare out of my sliding-glass doors. The moon is bright in the sky and lights up the tops of the pine trees. "Nah, it's only that the playoffs are so close. And he knows how many scouts will be there."

"So what's your top school?"

"Man, I don't even know. I just wanna go somewhere I can shine for a year. I'm trying to be one-and-done."

"Dang, big baller!" she says, her voice smiling at me hard through the phone, making me feel like I've already made it. "When you get to the NBA, you better not start acting brand-new!"

"First of all, brand-new? Nah, never that. And secondly, the statistical chances of me going to the league at all is about .03 percent, like three in every ten thousand dudes. So I'm not bettin' on it or anything," I tell Carli. But really,

I'm all *but* bettin' on it. I already know what team I want to play for. And no, it's not Los Angeles. I'm thinking San Antonio. Gregg Popovich's teams always seem like a family.

"Boy, don't play modest with me. You are not the average player. And you still have another year."

She's making me feel so good it's embarrassing. "But what about you? Don't you have dreams of playing in the league one day?" I ask to get the attention off of me. "I bet the top schools are already sending you letters. And you know they'll all be coming to the playoffs to see you in a few weeks, big baller!"

Carli goes quiet.

Damn, I forgot about the surgery. What if she won't be back in time for the playoffs? Great, just great. Here I am the asshole again.

CARLI

The stupid playoffs. I don't tell him I could care less about which scouts will be there because I don't want to play basketball anymore. I don't tell him that I'm more concerned with which color Le Pen to pull from my Pamela

Barsky canvas pencil pouch than being able to run up and down a court. He sounds way too excited, and I'm not ready to burst his bubble. I'm not ready to tell him that I don't love the game like he does.

"My bad. I wasn't even thinking about the surgery. What's the doctor saying about your chances of being ready for the playoffs?" he asks.

Periwinkle, I decide. I'm lying in my bed with my notebook, filling in the white space around *Rex Carrington* with the words *Numbers never really die* in multicolored columns. "Don't know. I have an appointment next week. Supposed to tell me then."

A text comes in from Jordan: **I'll get it back from him tomorrow. I swear**

You better, I text back. I can't believe this girl has lost the menu with the first kisses fact on the back. And I still can't find the original fact on my walls anywhere, so it's even more crucial for Jordan to find it. And no, I can't just write it again like she suggested. It wouldn't be the same.

For real, Jordan

Ok . . . ok

Earlier, Jordan's mom said she couldn't go to the game because she needed to study. So Jordan gave the menu to her brother to give to Cole to give to me. The problem is, her brother never gave it to Cole. When Cole didn't show up for shootaround, he gave it to Chico—this dude I used to date on Cole's team. Now, everybody and their mama know I dumped Chico over a month ago, but I guess Jordan's brother didn't get the memo.

So now the first sign on me and Rex's path is in the hands of a dude who doesn't know the difference between *they're, their,* and *there,* but who had the nerve to call me stupid for saying that crossing the train tracks on Westheimer at the exact same time it started pouring down hail (it was only pea-sized, but still!) was a sign that we should take a break.

"I'm sure you'll be good to go."

"What?"

"You know, good for the playoffs."

"I guess we'll see," I say. And then add, "But when can I see you, though?" to get on to more important things.

"When do you want to see me?" he says, putting some extra smooth sweetness in his voice, like he's spreading a layer of Nutella over his words. I can't even lie. . . . It's sexy.

"Like now. Like right now," I say, and laugh. "But I guess I could settle for this weekend."

"Look, I'll drive out there this second if you want me to."

"Yeah, whatever."

"No, I'm serious," he says.

My heart lights up at the possibility of seeing him. "You wouldn't get in trouble? You can sneak out this late without your parents noticing?"

"I wouldn't have to sneak. It's only my father and me, and he doesn't really care what I do," he answers in a voice that tells me he doesn't feel lucky to have so much freedom.

The hurt on his face earlier today jumps to the front of my mind, and I want to ask why his father doesn't care and where his mom is. But thinking about turning the conversation toward parents is making my own pain feel naked. A dark cloud swoops in, covers it, and I say, "Well, I'd definitely get in trouble. What about Friday?"

"I have a game on Friday. What about Saturday?" he asks.

"That works."

"Okay, text me your address."

My address. Dang, that's what Daddy called about earlier. Cole and I will be staying at his new rental house this weekend. But how can somewhere I've never been, somewhere Daddy doesn't belong, be my address?

Daddy's supposed to be lying on the sofa in our living room right now, watching SportsCenter. He's supposed to be standing in front of the stove tomorrow morning, whisking pancake mix in his big plastic bowl (the only plastic bowl in the house . . . Mom's tea is not the only thing she's bougie about). I swear sometimes I can still hear him shouting at the TV. I can smell his aftershave when I walk past the stove. But he's never there to reach out and hug me.

The cloud grows larger, but it's still not big enough to cover the pain. I put down my notebook and pen and gently reach for the lamp on my nightstand—cover myself in pitch darkness.

"I mean, not right now or anything. I can get it from you later."

"Huh?"

"Your address. No rush. We have all week," Rex explains.

"Yeah," I say, struggling for more words. Lying in bed with Rex on the other end of my phone should feel like heaven. But the darkness all around me, inside me, won't let me feel anything good. "I'm about to go to bed."

"Okay, talk tomorrow?"

"Yeah."

"And the day after that?"

"Yeah."

"And the day after that?"

A tiny sun peeks up from behind the cloud inside of me and I answer, "Yeah," smiling a little.

"And the day after that?"

More suns, rising higher. "Yeah, and the day after that," I say, and add a brief "bye" before hanging up, holding on to the good.

REX

Carli's street has a dope canopy of trees. Getting out of my pickup truck, I can't help but look up at the bright February sun peeking through the leaves of the large oak at the end of her driveway. Through the leaves of the oak beside it. And the one beside that, leaves wilding out in the wind. The sidewalk is lined with live oaks on both sides.

But walking up her driveway, I stop when I notice a sick magnolia tree alone in the middle of her yard. It makes me think about how trees like to grow close to each other. How they depend on each other. Sure, aboveground they may throw a few 'bows to get the most sun. But underground, they share—water, nitrogen, and nutrients—especially when one of them is suffering.

Even the strong trees, like the oak at the bottom of her driveway with the huge trunk and the mature crown stretching across the street, go through things. Even the strong ones do better when they're not alone.

CARLI

It's half past noon, and I'm sitting on the sofa in the living room of Daddy's rental house, which is way out in Woodside, closer to his job. Closer to Rex, too, who's supposed to be here any minute.

I should be happy that I'm here with Daddy, that I'm about to see Rex. But it feels weird having Rex come *here* to pick me up for the first time. To this foreign house, where he'll look at these foreign walls, walk on this foreign carpet, and sit on this foreign couch. And as if all this foreignness wasn't bad enough, everything is beige. It's like whoever decorated this house had a motto: *If it ain't beige, I ain't buying it.*

But apparently beige is the color of the universe. Yes, all the color of all the light of all the galaxies amounts to what scientists call *cosmic latte*—basically beige. Wouldn't think it, would you? Just found that fact on Google. I needed to find one good thing about this sad color around me, about this sad situation that led us to this sad house where Mom will never be. This bland house with no memories.

I write down the cosmic latte fact in my notebook with my brown Le Pen, cursive letters taking up most of the page, and draw small messy stars all around them, hoping they'll help light the way forward in this new house. Then I crease the paper around all four sides, folding it back and forth, and run my nail along the creases to make sure the paper tears clean.

Now that's a good rhombus! And I already know exactly where it needs to hang. I push myself off the sofa. Hard. Even harder because it's one of those sofas that tries to swallow you whole. Good thing my stomach is feeling better. No way I could've done this last week.

My new room is bare except for a bed underneath a large multipaned window, two cherry nightstands with iron scroll lamps, a matching dresser, and that life-sized poster of Candace Parker. I know, I know. I said she was coming down. But I didn't have the heart. Daddy was too proud of her. But you know what I *will* do? I'll pin this cosmic latte fact over the orange-and-white Spalding she's dribbling up the court.

Much better. Candace's yellow Los Angeles Sparks uniform will be next. Then her black knee braces, then her orange high-tops, and finally her black socks. Her face can stay. It would be a shame to cover such a determined face. Oooo, maybe I'll add a little speech bubble next to her mouth with a quote about those ancient penguins who grew to be almost seven feet tall.

The doorbell rings. Rex. If only I had the hospital menu to give to him today. But Chico claims he gave it to Cole, who claims he never got anything from Chico. So who knows where it's at now?

"I'll get it!" Cole shouts from the kitchen. He's been in there making snacks for Rex for the last hour.

Dang, can I be the one to answer the door? Rex *is* my date.

"Oh, is Rex here?" Daddy yells from his bedroom.

"Yeah," Cole shouts back. And by the time I walk out of my room, Cole is already whizzing past me to answer the door. I swear, Daddy and Cole have been entirely too excited about Rex coming today.

Cole swings opens the front door. "What up!" he says, and reaches to give Rex a hug.

● REX ●

Cole hugs me, and it feels like love. Carli, standing right behind him, smiles at me, and it feels like love. Carli's dad comes around a corner, filling out the hallway frame with his tall body, and it feels like love.

Hold up. I'm not used to this. My father doesn't give two shits about me—fact. No need to sugarcoat it. And sure, Angie checks for me. But at first, she was paid to. And she has the people she's never been paid to care for waiting for her at home. Also fact. And no girl has ever truly cared about me. Maybe the basketball me, but never the real me.

And now it's like a few people are showing me a little love and I'm losing it. Filling up with way too many feelings, way too fast. I cannot, will not, start crying again. Crying in front of Carli once was enough. Twice in less than a week *and* in front of her family? Nah, dawg, I'm not *even* going out like that.

"Derek," her dad says, sidestepping Carli for a handshake—weaker than what I expected coming from a man even taller than I am.

Carli rolls her eyes, only a little bit but I still catch it.

She's standing behind him, sliding her small, gold medallion back and forth across its chain.

Her dad continues, "Carli tells me you live close. Hope it wasn't too hard to find."

"Nah, not at all." I say.

Carli playfully throws up her hands and says, "Dang, is it my turn now?"

Man, does she look good. She's wearing this faded black 2Pac T-shirt under a pale purple cardigan, some ripped jeans, and her burgundy Blazers. Doesn't even look like she has on makeup. Not that she needs any.

I take advantage of her open arms to get up in there for a hug. I don't want to hug her too tight now. Not with her surgery. And not with Cole and her dad standing right here watching, either. But her hair. I forgot how good it smells. It's like putting my face in a hedge of jasmine. I take two deep breaths, forgetting all about the audience.

Carli lets go of me. "Come," she says, and takes my hand.

We sit on the sofa, situated in front of three large windows, and I sink into its softness. I'd almost forgotten what it feels like to sit on a comfortable couch. It feels like home.

Without telling us to pose, Cole snaps a pic of Carli

and me with his phone and then says, "Made some fresh guacamole and lemonade. Want some?"

"Do I?" I say, smiling. Love me some guacamole. Makes all of the frozen taquitos and burritos I eat feel like a real meal. And I must say, my guacamole goes hard. Cole better come with it.

"Hope you can take a little heat. I make mine spicy."

"Trust, I can take the heat. I make mine with jalapeño *and* serrano," I respond.

"All right, then," Cole says, and disappears into the kitchen.

"Hope you can take all this attention," Carli says, and widens her eyes, "because *damn!*"

"I have something I want to show y'all," Carli's dad says excitedly, like he has big news. He's standing up in front of the TV with two remotes in hand. Once he gets Apple TV up on the screen, he settles into the love seat beside a big fake tree.

Can somebody please tell me the point of fake trees? They don't give oxygen. They don't clean the air. They're frauds. Who wants to be looking at a fraud every day? But I try not to let the fake tree bother me. This house is only temporary anyway. Carli said her mom and dad are just taking a breather. A little space for a few months, then her dad is gonna move back in this summer.

Carli is up on the screen. Ah, man. Look at her. Can't be more than six or seven with a million twists, and she's dribbling a basketball. Even that young, the girl had handles.

"Daddy!" Carli protests. "Really?"

"It's not too long, I promise," her dad says, staring at the screen, eyes wide and full of pride.

Carli rolls hers, but I don't know why. I can't imagine my father looking at me the way her dad looks at her. I can't imagine my father taking the time to do something this special for me.

The montage of videos and photos moves from year to year, uniform to uniform, and hairstyle to hairstyle with Carli dribbling, shooting, stealing balls, breaking away for layups, headlining newspapers, accepting awards, and— wait. That's me.

At a basketball camp hosted by the Houston Rockets when I was eight. How did he find that picture? I've never even seen it. And me again, winning my first AAU championship when I was, like, ten. Angie took that same pic from a different angle. Newspaper clippings, team photos, and online articles from over the years. The times I made the highlight reel on ESPN.

I can't believe he did all of this for me. He doesn't even know me. Damn, here it comes again. This feeling of love, filling me up, trying to spill over. I blink it back.

Cole walks in with a tray of guacamole, chips, and lemonade, and I'm over the brim. A tear falls down my right cheek, and I wipe it quick. But not before Carli sees. I let go of her hand and stand up.

"Excuse me for a minute," I say, trying to hold my voice steady and get up out of there.

CARLI

"Not cool," I say, and stand up. "Rex is my date. *Mine.* Y'all around here trippin' over him so hard that y'all scared him off." I walk over to the front door. "I swear if y'all have messed this up for me—" I can't think of anything to complete the threat, so I repeat, "I swear," and walk out, annoyed I'm not dramatic enough to slam the door behind me.

Outside it's bright and cool. Rex is standing near the big tree in the center of the yard.

"Your magnolia has scale," he says.

"Yeah?" I say, not really knowing what he's talking about. I walk onto the freshly cut grass, crunching beneath my Blazers, to be with him.

"The infestation is pretty bad. It needs to be sprayed." He runs his fingers along the branch of the tree and starts picking off some gross-looking white stuff.

It's a pretty tree, I'll admit, with its huge, waxy leaves and white flowers. But this is not my tree or my house. "We're not going to be living here that long."

"I know, but if the tree doesn't get treatment, it'll die," he says like it's a big problem. Like it's my big problem.

"Okaaaay." Look, I don't want the tree to die, I really don't. But I also don't have time to be worried about a random tree right now. "Why you so worried about a tree?"

● REX ●

I really don't want to be this dude. This crying-ass dude. Where did he come from? I've been going through life *cool*. Sure, I have a father who hates me and a dead mom, but that's been the case from day one. And I've been *cool*.

But it seems like ever since I met Carli, this dude keeps creepin' up on me. I came out here to get away from him. Started telling Carli about the scale on the tree to *keep* away from him. But here he comes again.

"Trees make me feel close to my mom," I say, truth pouring out of me. I pick at the scale on a small limb, trying to keep the crying-ass dude away.

"Where is she?" Carli asks, and interlaces her fingers with mine. She starts to walk.

I let go of the limb and walk with her, off the grass and onto the sidewalk. "She died," I say.

"I'm so sorry," she says, looks over at me, and squeezes my hand.

I want to kiss her. Yeah, the timing might seem a little weird, but I need something to help me kick this dude to the curb. It's time for him to go.

But before I can stop and lean in, Carli says, "Can I ask how she died? How old were you?"

I start to overflow. I mean, I'm crying hard. Right in front of Carli.

Carli stops walking and turns toward me. "It's okay," she says, and brushes my cheeks with her thumbs.

But it's not okay. Not only is it ridiculously embarrassing

to be crying like this, I've never talked about what happened to Mom to anyone. Not even Angie. Sure, we've talked about her, but never what happened to her.

Carli grabs my hand and starts walking again.

I look down at my blurred, black-and -red Jordans—one in front of the other, in front of the other, on white concrete. I am dude and dude is me. There's no getting away from him or the answer to Carli's questions. It's banging around inside me like it wants to be free. Like it's been waiting to come out since the day I figured out what I'd done.

I was four and Angie was showing me a stack of old pictures she'd found. Mom pregnant at the park. Mom pregnant at a museum. Mom pregnant in the living room. Mom pregnant at the hospital. And then the pictures ran out.

But do I really have to admit out loud to killing Mom? I admit it to myself every day. I tell Mom I'm sorry every morning when I wake up and every night before I go to sleep. I ask her for forgiveness every time I go to the free-throw line. I hate myself for it. Isn't that enough? But the banging is getting stronger, blurred J after blurred J, and then looking into Carli's teary eyes.

"She died giving birth to me," I admit to her. "Yeah, I'm the asshole who killed his own mom."

CARLI

"Don't say that. You're not an asshole," I tell him. But the tight squeeze of his closed eyes and the low hang of his long jaw tells me he doesn't believe me. I wrap my arms around his waist and bury my head in the crook of his neck, hoping to drive some of his pain away.

He hugs me back and cries into my hair.

"It's not your fault," I tell him. "You were a newborn."

He lets out a low moan, and it vibrates through my body—baby explosions of pain. They make me feel like I'm dying.

Oh my God. Is this what Rex feels like? I can't even imagine. My pain doesn't even come close to his. At least both of my parents are still alive. Just thinking about it makes me feel grateful. And for half a second, I half forget about Rex's pain and feel happy.

Seriously, Carli? How could I possibly feel anything good when Rex is feeling so bad?

Oh no! Panic rings through my body like a three a.m. burglar alarm. What if Rex just felt my happiness like I could feel his pain? How could I even begin to explain?

But it wasn't me. It was gratitude.

The truth never sounded so stupid.

Part of me waits for him to push me away, but he pulls me in even closer. And I'm so relieved I could cry. But the relief doesn't last long in the swarming guilt, under the crushing weight, where it's a strain to find my next breath.

We can't stay here.

I take in a slow, deep breath—my belly pressing against Rex's trembling belly—and let it out. Again. And again, until the trembling stops. Until his belly finally pushes firmly into mine and falls away. Until his breath picks up the pace of my own—now warm and moist on my face.

I lift my head out of the hot crook of his neck toward the bright blue sky. So cool and sweet I have to close my eyes. When I open them, Rex is looking up, too. I take it as a sign that he's okay and start walking again.

At the corner I guide us left. Daddy says there's a park up here. Figure it'll be a nice to sit on some swings and chill out for a little while.

"Y'all got a court over here?" Rex exclaims, face lit up like a kid on Christmas. He reclaims his arm from around my shoulder and picks up the pace.

I look for a basketball court but can't see it. Then, just above a thick hedge ahead, I spot a slither of orange hoop. How did he even see that?

We cross the street, Rex with extra pep in his step. It's crazy how much spotting the court lifted his mood. It's like the whole breakdown over his mom never even happened. Who knew basketball was out here working miracles like this?

"Man, I've been looking for a court out here for the *longest*," he says excitedly. "They got this joint hidden! You know white people don't like basketball courts in their neighborhoods . . . attracts too many of us," Rex says, and rubs the top of his brown hand with his pointer finger. He's walking so fast I can barely keep up. "Well, guess what? We found the secret court and we're tellin' *all* our friends!" He laughs. "Wait, I don't really have any friends," he says, and turns back toward me. "But now at least I have you."

We walk through a small opening in the thick hedge.

"No friends?" I ask, looking around the secret park. No swings. Just the court to the left and an open field in the back. Leave it to Daddy to find the only public basketball court in Woodside.

"Nah, not really." He walks ahead of me, then turns around so that he's walking backward, facing me. He brings his hands up to eye level, about body-width apart, and moves them in sync—right to left, left to right, right to left—like windshield wipers or something. It's strange. "I guess there's Dante and Paul, two of the dudes I used to ball with at the court close to my old neighborhood. But once I moved out here, I haven't seen them. Same with Craig and James, two of my old teammates who were pretty cool."

He pushes his arms toward the sky, flicks his right wrist, and I see it. The follow-through. The invisible basketball. I don't know why I didn't see it sooner. Jordon's always playing with hers.

"And forget about any of my new teammates."

"So, who do you hang with then?" I ask, hoping he's had somebody before me. Everybody needs somebody.

But his feet have already hit the court. A huge smile flashes across his face before he turns around and takes off running, dribbling his invisible ball. Approaching the goal, he crosses over left, dribbles between his legs, and goes up for a windmill dunk—head almost hitting the rim. When he lands, he shouts, "What! These fools can't hold me . . . they can't stop me!"

 REX

Carli's walking up to the three-point line, looking at me like I'm half-crazy. Okay, maybe the yelling was a little much.

But when it comes to basketball, I go straight beast mode. I can't help myself.

"Carli Alexander has the ball," I say in my commentator voice, trying to take the attention off me, and chest pass her the invisible ball.

Her arms stay by her sides. She doesn't even try to catch it.

"Oh, so you're not playing with me?" I ask, standing underneath the rim, dramatically throwing up my hands.

She cracks a small smile, playfully rolls her eyes, runs to get the ball, and dribbles it back toward me. "Happy now?"

"Yes," I answer, mostly because it's good to see her run. I knew she was feeling better, but not that much better.

She bounce passes the ball back to me.

"That's all you got?"

"Yep."

"What about that behind-the-back move you did with all those ponytails? Man, that was sick." I bounce pass the ball back to her.

She catches it. "Ugh, I'd almost forgotten about that. I can't believe my dad. I'm so sorry. He's a bit of a basketball freak and he's—"

"Are you kidding me? I loved it!" I say, walking toward her. "Seeing you ball way back in the day and the old footage of me was everything. I swear your dad is the best. My father would never." And I stop right there. Not about to give her two sob stories in one day.

She dribbles toward me. "Seriously? My dad makes videos like that all the time. *So* annoying. But I must admit, I liked seeing you when you were little. Too cute." She backs into me, still dribbling.

Behind her, I swipe like I'm trying to steal the ball.

"I can send you the video if you want," she says before dribbling left.

I was hoping she'd offer. "That'd be cool," I say, arms extended wide in my defensive stance. She goes up for a layup and I put both of my arms straight up in the air. Nobody gets an easy shot. Not even just-had-surgery Carli. Yeah, I'm savage like that.

"Oh, it's like that?" she asks, getting up in my face after she makes her layup.

I step closer to her. So close our bodies are touching and I'm getting lost in the patch of freckles around her nose, in her smiling brown eyes. "Yeah, it's like that."

CARLI

The way Rex is looking at me . . . it's like he knows everything about me. Everything that ever was. Everything that will ever be.

Looking straight into his dark, tender eyes, all I want to do is lose myself to the infinite parts of me that he sees and forget about what's actually going on in my life. But the way he just opened up and poured out all his pain makes me feel bad for keeping so many secrets.

But it's too late, I think. I've already lied, omitted so much truth. He can't know I could lie to him. He needs someone to trust, someone to be his friend, someone to help heal his hurts. *I can be all of that,* I tell myself. *I can be his everything.*

"What?" he asks.

"Nothing," I say, and kiss him. Pressing my lips into his big, soft lips is way easier than admitting my parents are getting a divorce and I have to decide which one to live with. And rolling my tongue over and around his tongue is way better than letting him know I plan to quit basketball.

He pulls me in closer, his strong hand pressing into my back, making me feel things in low places. Low places that want to explode. Then he pulls away and looks me in the eyes. "I'm so happy I met you," he says.

"Me, too," I say, head tilted back, looking at his face. It's radiating with adoration—for me. I take in as much of it as I can, whole skies of it, hoping it will stay with me forever.

He briefly kisses me again. "Seriously, my life is so much better with you in it."

"Mine, too."

"Carli," he says, looking straight into my eyes.

Words cannot even touch the happiness I feel . . . here . . . with him . . . under the light of the winter sun. Happiness in a way I've never felt before. "Yes," I answer.

"Who's recruiting you?"

Hold up a second. How did we get on basketball?

"I know Texas probably is. UConn, Stanford, Vanderbilt, Duke? You're probably getting recruited by the top schools in the country. Tell me I'm wrong."

I don't, because he's not.

"I know I'm getting way ahead of myself. Waaaaay. It's a whole year out. But wouldn't it be cool if we lived in the same city after we graduated? At least the same state. Trust, you'd have front-row seats to every game you could make. And you'd better have some seats with my name on them, too. I could even visit you at your dorm. Kick your roommate to the curb for a little bit," he says, and laughs.

"Yeah," I say, feeling his words flying around inside me with no place to land. Most of the schools recruiting me will be off the table if I don't play basketball. Who knows where I'll end up?

College applications are due next January. I need to start working on them this fall, but which ones? If I want to study astronomy, Vassar and Vanderbilt have cool observatories. If I want to be some type of artist or designer, RISD or Parsons would be good choices. If I want to be a writer, Northwestern and Brown have good creative writing programs. If I want to be some type of historian, UCLA would be a good option. It's not like I haven't done the research. The signs just haven't spoken yet. *But what exactly am I supposed to do about that? I've done everything I can!* I want to yell from the top of my lungs. I want to tell him everything.

But I don't. And it feels miserable. It's like all of Rex's pain got to go outside and play in the rain—with everything we feel, with his dreams—until the sun came out. But all of my pain is still stuck inside, staring through rain-streaked windows at everyone playing.

BUBBLES
OF
HOPE

CARLI

Mom pulls into the lot behind her design studio. We just got back from my two-week checkup, where I got the worst news. Dr. Williams advised easing back into playing over the next day or so but said that I should be able to go full force for the first round of the playoffs next Saturday.

"So that's it? You just want me to show up for practice on Monday and start playing again?" I say, rubbing my hands together in front of the vents of her old Land Rover Discovery. I swear it took the whole drive over here for the heat to kick in. I've *been* telling Mom she needs a new car. She's had this thing since before I was born but refuses to give it up. Says she likes the old body style. I'd take good heat and not having to stop at a gas station every three seconds, but that's me.

"Well, you know, Dr. Williams *did* clear you to play," she says, and starts wrapping an oversized mustard-yellow scarf around her neck.

"Maybe she doesn't know what she's talking about. I could go back to play too soon and rip my stomach apart," I say, annoyed at my own high-pitched, whiny voice.

Mom grabs her phone and keys out of one of the cupholders in the center console and says, "Okay." But it's not a you're-right okay. It's more like a you're-being-ridiculous okay. Doesn't she know I can hear the difference?

"I'm serious, Mom! I bet you won't be so nonchalant when my stomach rips open." Then I remember Mom and me getting down to old-school Ciara this morning in the kitchen before she took me to the doctor. I had the nerve to drop down into the splits. Yes, the splits! With ease, like I never even had surgery. I'm telling you, technology has gotten too advanced for its own damn good.

"Not sure how that's gonna happen. The puncture wounds were so tiny you didn't even need stitches."

Oooo, I hate when Mom calmly throws out facts when all I'm trying to do is pitch a fit.

"And honestly, Carli," Mom says, reaching into the backseat for her neon-yellow Cambridge satchel, "I don't see any reason you shouldn't finish the season if you're physically able." She throws her phone and keys into the bag.

"But you know I hate basketball!"

"Yes, but the championship game is only . . . what? Two weeks away. And that's if your team keeps winning. Either way, it will all be over soon. After that, you can choose a different direction. You have a lot to think about, you know." She lifts her portable tea infuser from the cupholder closest to her and takes a sip.

"Yeah, how can I forget?"

"Come on," she says, and opens the car door, cold air blasting my face. Late February, and winter finally decides to show up in Houston. It's freaking thirty-one degrees. I swear everything wants to be on my nerves today.

We walk through the back door and down a hall lined with tiny, glass-front offices. It's been forever since I've been in here. I don't recognize any of the girls behind their white, modern desks, staring at their large Mac screens. But their white, pushpin walls, covered by all things interior design, are just as cool as I remember.

One office rushes at me with color and patterns—a photo of a cobalt-blue sofa below a turquoise chandelier; a sample of a hot pink, orange, and gold rug; and swatches of diamond-patterned fabrics. I stop walking and look inside. On the back wall there are photos of beautifully tiled Moroccan arches and columns. *This house is gonna be dope,* I think, before the Emma Watson–looking girl behind the desk, with a brown pixie cut and dark red lips, looks up. She sees Mom, grabs a folder off her desk, springs out of her chair, and quickly tiptoes around the intricately carved cream tile organized on the concrete floor.

She swings her glass door open, says "Hey, Carli," like she knows me, and runs to catch up with Mom.

"Mrs. Alexander!" calls a different girl, from somewhere behind me.

I turn around like she's calling me, like I'm the boss. And for a second, my neck gets long, my shoulders roll back, and I'm feeling myself. Like I'm doing it big and I have life all worked out. Then she runs past me to secure her position on the other side of Mom and bursts my little bubble.

The front of the store opens up to the retail shop with its teal-framed floor-to-ceiling windows enticing everyone passing by on Westheimer Road to come on in. Oh my God, it smells so good in here. And I see why. There's a long rectangular table full of candles. I pick up one with two small crystals sitting on either side of its wick.

"That's the moon batch candle, hand poured only during full moons," says the guy behind the hammered gold checkout desk. He's a young black dude wearing a multicolored, silky, patched jacket. Sounds ugly, but it's super cute. There's a huge yellow *G* on the front, left side of the jacket above a patch that reads *Men at Work*. And the right sleeve is full of bright blue stars of all different sizes.

"Cool, I'll take one," I say, and then add, "Cute jacket."

"Thanks, made it myself," he replies.

I can't believe how much the shop has changed. Mom used to sell only home accessories, but now there are kimono robes, leather totes, woven pouches, handmade jewelry, fancy chocolate, notebooks, gold engraved pencils, and wait— There's a whole wall of greeting cards. I walk closer to see what they're talking about.

You have the trying-to-be-cool section with sayings like *Yaas Queen* and *Birthday Squad* printed over graphic images. Then you have the legitimately beautiful section with intricate designs and lots of gold leaf. There's even a whole collage section. A sympathy card with cut-out footprints in the sand. A congratulations card with cut-out champagne flutes. Come on, now. I could do better than that.

The best one is a printed collage of a girl standing in a long T-shirt holding a bouquet of peach flowers over her face. In the background are planets, stars, a dog on its hind legs wearing a party hat, and the words *dance to your own music . . . it's your birthday.* My birthday is not until November, but this card absolutely belongs on my walls next to the watercolor I did in art class last year. A bouquet of balloons high in the sky carrying a baby elephant—the only other mammal that knows how to dance.

At the checkout desk, the guy with the cute jacket asks, "Are you adding this to your mom's account?"

I guess everyone in here knows who I am. "No, that's okay," I say. Mom and Daddy always stress the importance of me and Cole budgeting for what we want. Plus, I have plenty of money in my checking account. We've both had accounts since we were ten. That's where Mom and Daddy deposit our allowance. And I like to see my money stack. I mean, I spend money on magazines and the occasional cute top or jumpsuit or whatever I find in thrift shops. But that's it.

"You sure?" he asks, his bright blue-lined eyes looking confused.

"Yeah, I'm good." I reply, and pull my phone out of my back pocket for Apple Pay. There's a missed text from Rex asking how the doctor's appointment went. I don't *even* feel like thinking about that.

And there's a missed group text from Daddy asking to stop by tonight. Mom has already responded with *OK*. Cole responded with 👍 🖤 😊 My heart lifts and twirls in my chest at the thought of the whole family being together again. I can't help but think it's a sign that there's still hope.

REX

Sitting in my pickup truck in the parking lot after school, heat on blast trying to warm up, I check my phone again. Still no response from my father. Took me all week to work up the nerve to send him that video Carli's dad made. Each time I'd load the video into our conversation—where my last message, **1st game of season tonight at 7 if you wanna come**, still sat unanswered—I'd delete it.

But this morning, I loaded it, typed, **What I've been up to all these years**, and quickly pressed Send.

When I checked my phone at lunch and he hadn't replied, I added, **Oh that's my new girlfriend. She can ball too**.

And after fifth period, when he still hadn't replied, I texted, **And she's dope in a million other ways**.

Now that school's over and he still hasn't replied, I type, **Not that you care**. But something inside me won't let me press Send. Something stupid and weak and still hopeful. You'd think that after all these years, I'd be all out of hope. Nope, not my dumb ass.

I ring Carli. She still hasn't texted me back from earlier. I want to know how her doctor's appointment went, but she doesn't pick up. *Damn, did the doctor tell her she couldn't play?*

Coach gave us a rare day off—no practice, no game, no team meeting, nothing. Said we needed rest before the playoffs. But it's hard to rest when I don't know what's up with my girl.

When I get back to the crib, my father's Tesla is parked in the driveway. His sneakers and messenger bag are haphazardly tossed by the front door. The house is toasty. And I can hear the TV playing in the living room. It feels like home. So much so that I want to drop my backpack and yell, "Dad, I'm home!" like people do in the movies. But my mouth acts like it doesn't know how to move.

And my body isn't doing any better. Instead of heading to the living room, I'm standing frozen in the foyer with my arms folded across my chest, feeling like . . . It's hard to explain.

Man, do you know how many times I've hoped to come home to my father sitting in the living room? How many times I've psyched myself into thinking, *Today is the day.* The day he'll be chillin' on the sofa when I get home and I'll join him, and we'll chop it up and maybe even bust out a bag of potato chips. Now today really could be that day. It definitely feels like that day. But what if it isn't?

Well, it wouldn't be anything new. I don't have anything to lose, I convince myself, and take off my coat and shoes and put them away in the mudroom. Then I take as much air as I can into my lungs and blow it out slow before walking down the hall and turning the corner.

I don't see my father, but he must be around here somewhere. A clip from my freshman year is playing on our ridiculously large flat-screen. Not one from the video Carli's dad made. Must be YouTube or something. And I'm right on time to see my younger self cock the ball back and posterize somebody.

"Damn, your boy is cold!" I say, out loud to myself. In case you haven't noticed, your boy is prone to referring to himself in third person. Makes talking to himself more fun.

But this time there's a response. "You really are," my father says in his soft voice, and sits up on the sofa. He looks back at me, eyes red and puffy, like he's been crying. Actually, he's still crying.

And once again I can't move or speak. This moment

should feel good, right? In my head, my father watching me play, giving me praise, and shedding tears for me is like heaven.

But standing ten feet from the man who ignored me all these years and actually hearing his words and seeing his tears is different. It's all kinds of shock and hope and sadness and love and hurt and anger and hate—yes, hate—pushing up inside me all at once, trying to get out.

I don't know whether I want to run to him or away from him. Whether I want to punch him in the face or hug him. I just don't know.

"Why did I buy this sofa?" he asks, and reaches around to rub his back. "They shouldn't even be able to call this thing a sofa."

Of *all* things for him to say. It's weird. I think if he would've said, *Sorry*, or something like that, my hate would've come raging out. But I could feel him on the sofa tip—deeply. "Man! I. Don't. Know," I reply. "That sofa is trash. All the seating in this house is trash."

"It really is. We need new furniture, stat. I want to be out here—"

"Word," I interrupt, "like yesterday." I'm not ready for everything he has to say. Not yet. I walk a few steps closer but don't go sit down.

"Let's do it. This time you can pick it out. Clearly I don't know what I'm doing."

"Bet! Carli's mom is a designer. I'm sure she could hook the house up," I say before realizing he doesn't know who Carli is. "Carli's my girlfriend."

"Figured that," he says, and guiltily shifts his eyes away from me. "The one from the video you sent?"

"Yeah," I say, trying to pretend that our everything-is-cool bubble just didn't crack, trying to pretend that him not knowing Carli's name or not really knowing who I am or never seeing me ball or him refusing to love me all these years doesn't hurt, doesn't piss me off.

I walk over to the kitchen to get myself some apple juice. "Want some juice?" I call out to my father to try to repair the crack. I'm good with the everything-is-cool bubble for now. Nah, I *need* the bubble right now.

"Yes, please," my father says. "And can you heat up a couple of those arepas?"

"Arepas! Angie was here again?"

"Yep."

"Man, Angie's arepas go so hard."

"Don't they?"

And just like that, we're back in there.

CARLI

When we pull up to the house, Daddy's Tahoe is parked in the middle of the driveway.

"Now, why would he do that?" Mom says, and parks on the street.

"Probably wasn't thinking." I defend Daddy, even though I'm mad we'll have to walk in the cold instead of going straight into the house from the garage. But right now, it's not about me. If Mom and Daddy have any chance of reconciling today, she can't start off with an attitude. "You need help carrying anything?" I ask Mom to try to help better her mood.

"Yeah, can you grab those plans off the backseat? Thanks."

I turn around, get on my knees, and grab two giant rolls of architectural plans. *Barbara A*, the name of Mom's interior design business (her first name and middle initial), is stamped in red on the outside. "Are these for the new boutique?"

"Sure are," she says, smiling. "We start the build-out next month."

Inside, Daddy's keys are in the singing bowl on the side table near the front door. I stop and smile at them for a second before going into the breakfast room where he and Cole are at the table playing chess on our vintage chessboard. Well, actually, Daddy looks like he's trying to decide his next move and Cole is taking pictures. Not even with his iPhone; he brought out the Nikon—the big dog. He's probably thinking the same thing I am—*There's hope!*

"Hey," Cole says, and comes to give me a hug. But he has on entirely too much cologne. Don't know what girl he was trying to impress, but he's not about to have me smelling like that.

I duck his arms. "Dang, bathe in cologne much?"

Cole pinches his shirt as if poppin' his collar. "Don't hate. Appreciate," he says, and laughs.

"Brought some Ethiopian food," Daddy says, and stands up out of the deep-seated bench flanking the window.

Behind him the wind whips through the big tree in the backyard, making the antique brass bells hanging from its branches softly ring out.

"It's in there on the island," he adds.

He knows Ethiopian is Mom's favorite. *There's definitely hope.*

Mom looks over at the white plastic bags sitting on the kitchen island—teal with a butcher-block countertop. "Thanks, just give me a minute to put all this down," she says, referring to the stack of catalogs she's carrying.

"I'll get 'em," Cole says, offering to take them from her.

"No, it's fine," she says, and walks past the kitchen and down the hall to her office.

Before I hug Daddy, I place the plans down on the table next to the chessboard. Man-oh-man-oh-man, does it feel good to be hugging him in our house.

"What are these?" Daddy says, and lets go of me. He reaches down for one.

Oh shit! He's not supposed to know about the new boutique. "Oh, just some old plans," I lie, hoping it ends there.

But it doesn't. He slides the green rubber band off one of the rolls and takes a look.

"Why you being so nosy?" I ask, trying to play it off.

Daddy spreads the plans out on the table.

Cole walks over to take a look, too. "Oh, what's this going to be?" he asks excitedly. "A bar? A restaurant?" Mom has designed several of those. Cole gets closer. "Big rounders . . . tiny squares . . . small rounders . . . rectangles everywhere. Oh, I see. It's a boutique. It's cool the way it's set up," he says, running his fingers along the blue lines. He's always been able to easily read plans. But he's terrible at reading the room. Can't he see Daddy standing here fuming?

"Yeah, looks like your mom is opening another shop," Daddy says.

"Oh, cool. I didn't even know. Expanding! Go, Mom!" Cole says, still clueless.

Daddy sits back on the bench, crosses his arms, and starts

biting the inside of his cheek near his bottom lip. He's pissed.

Cole finally notices that something is up, and his face drains of excitement.

Mom walks into the kitchen and gets four plates down from the cabinet. She hasn't even looked at Daddy.

I go help, taking four sets of silverware out of the drawer near the dishwasher. We are soooo close to having a family dinner. All of us together, sitting around the table, talking and sharing.

"You know what?" Daddy starts, and stands up. The crease above the bridge of his nose is deep, his eyebrows low, and his nostrils are flared.

Mom looks up at him. She's holding two glass tumblers that she just got down from the cabinet.

"I came over here to apologize. For everything. For creating this whole mess. But then I see this. You want to talk about my secrets, but you have yours, too, *Barbara A*." Daddy's voice is loud and harsh, and the emphasis on Mom's business name is nasty.

Cole and I exchange glances. He already looks ready to cry. But I'm sitting up here wondering about secrets. I mean, I know all about Mom's secret. And yeah, she should have told Daddy about the new boutique, but Daddy *stays* trippin' about how much she works. It's not like he was about to be supportive. But what are Daddy's secrets?

Mom doesn't say anything. She places the two glasses on the counter and reaches to get one more (there goes our family dinner). I wish she would at least say something.

"Okay, okay," Daddy continues, his face red. "You want to sit up here and ignore me? Well, I'm filing for sole custody. Let's see how well you can ignore that."

"That's absurd," Mom says, like it's a fact, and starts unpacking the Ethiopian food.

"I have grounds," Daddy says, turning on his lawyer voice. "With the new store, you'll never be home. Hell, you were never home before. You can visit the kids at my house if you want."

"Visit? My kids?" Mom responds, her voice going uncharacteristically high. Daddy's last comments definitely got her attention. "I think it's time for you to leave," she says, her voice returning to normal. "I hope you're not serious."

"Oh, I'm dead serious," Daddy says, walking toward the door. "And by the way," he says, turning back and directing his attention toward me and Cole, "I found a house in the same neighborhood where the rental house is. So, if y'all come live with me, y'all can go to Woodside High."

"With Rex?" Cole asks, as if that makes everything better.

"Rex! Who cares about Rex right now!" I yell, and run to my room.

✳ REX ✳

It's freezing and I've been standing outside of Carli's heavily studded, powder-blue front door for entirely too long. I lift the ring on the large metal knocker. *I shouldn't be here,* I think for the hundredth time.

See, Carli didn't exactly invite me over. Actually, she didn't invite me at all and still hasn't returned any of my calls. And she's never told me where her mom's house is. Cole's photo tags on IG helped me find the street—quiet and tree-lined in South Hampton near Rice University. And their mom's old-school Discovery parked outside helped me pinpoint the house. It consistently appears in Cole's feed.

Yo, this is waaay too stalkerish. What am I thinking? I gently set the knocker back down without making a sound and put my hands in my coat pockets to warm them up.

"Ugh." I sigh, frustrated with myself, and a cloud of my breath hits the door. I swear it's braver than I am.

But I'm not getting back in my pickup truck without seeing Carli, you can bet on that. I need to make sure she's okay. Assure her that missing the playoffs is not the end of the world. Plus, this crazy good day with my father won't be the same if I don't share it with her.

The door starts making unlocking sounds from the inside. Shit! I want to run, but there's no time! I look for somewhere to hide on the long porch, but there's only the hanging swing and two large pots with unhappy succulents. It's too cold for them to be outside.

The door opens. The same tall woman with short hair from the hospital is about to walk out of the house with a thick blanket wrapped around her. But when she sees me, she stops and narrows the opening in the door. She looks at me—alarmed.

Oh, wait. She doesn't know me. "Hi, I'm Rex," I hurry up and say.

"So *you're* Rex," she says, like she's been hearing things about me.

"Yes, ma'am."

"No need for *ma'am*s," she says, and widens the door. "Why don't you come in."

"Thanks," I say, and step in, feeling my body relax into the warmth. I swear, the insides of a house have never felt or smelt so good. It's like the toffee candy Angie used to make mixed with her morning coffee with a little bit of Christmas and a dash of lavender. Don't forget about the vanilla. It's like the scents never end.

Carli's mom closes the door and says, "I'm Barbara,"

extending her hand out from underneath the blanket to shake mine.

"A pleasure to meet you," I say as politely as I can.

"Carli!" she shouts over her shoulder, "Rex is here!" Then she turns back to me and asks, "So, you go to school with Carli?"

"No, I go to Woodside High."

"I see," she says, and nods.

Carli comes walking down the hall in a long NASA T-shirt hiding everything underneath. What exactly? My eyes are begging to know. They look closer and I tell them to stop, but they're like hardheaded kids. They've never seen so much of her skin. The strong curve of her calves, the light spots dotting her right shin and knee (I wonder what those are), the dark bruise on her left thigh (I wonder how she got that), the way her thighs get paler and thicker, much thicker, as they reach higher toward the shirt. My eyes turn things over to my head and I wonder what her thighs look like higher, even higher—*hot damn.*

"It's so cold," Carli says, hugging herself as she nears the doorway. She looks confused, like she's wondering what I'm doing here, and her usual brightness is strained behind sad eyes.

Damn, I feel awful. I'm standing here eyeing her up, not even thinking about the whole reason I came over in the first place. I can't imagine having to sit out the rest of the season and missing the playoffs. I wish I could wrap my arms around her and tell her it's going to be okay. But I don't want to do all that in front of her mom, so I say, "Yeah, it is."

"Well, maybe you should go put some clothes on," her mom says, and gives her a look.

Carli rolls her eyes. "I have clothes on," she says, and raises her shirt to show some small drawstring shorts.

"Barely," her mom replies.

"Really, Mom?" Carli whines, widening her eyes.

"Fine, I'm going out to put the Rover in the garage."

"Okaaay," Carli says in a way that sounds like, *Why you telling me?*

I'm so embarrassed I could disappear. Sad or not, that was rude as hell.

Her mom tilts her head, shifts her neck back, and gives Carli a look. I don't need a mom to know that look. When a woman starts using neck action, shit is real.

"Sorry," Carli says, and softens her eyes. "It's just—"

"I know," her mom interrupts, returning the soft look, and adds, "It's okay," before hitting the unlock button on a car key, tightening the blanket around herself, and dashing outside.

I scoop Carli up in my arms.

She hugs my neck and sighs, breath hot and sticky with hurt.

"It's okay. Everything is going to be okay," I say, holding her.

She sighs again and slides her long body down mine. "What are you doing here? How'd you even know where I live?"

But before I can come up with an answer, she gently takes my hand and leads me farther into the warm house with its old wooden floors and colorful rugs and clusters of sweet-smelling candles burning on every table. Past paintings and masks and maps and mirrors and framed photos hanging on white walls. Past the living room with its velvet burnt-orange sofa and floor-to-ceiling books on recessed shelves. (Man, I would kill to live in this house.) And down the hall to her room.

CARLI

I close the door to my room, lean back against it, and grab Rex's hands—still cold. I bring him closer to me, rub my nose against the tip of his nose—even colder. Rub my left cheek against his, back and forth, until his warms.

"Damn, how long were you standing out there?" I say, and give him a kiss.

"A *minute*," he says, "a long minute."

"Sorry, I didn't know you were coming. What are you even doing here?"

He's looking around at my walls. "Well, Cole—"

"Oh my gosh. I'm so stupid. Of course it was Cole," I say, feeling my upper lip hike up. If Cole thinks inviting Rex over tonight is about to make me peace out Mom, he has another thing coming.

"No, no. I just wanted to make sure you were okay. Tried calling and texting but hadn't heard from you," Rex says, and lowers the black hoodie off his head, his face holding space for everything good and sweet.

I kiss him again. Regardless of Cole's motivation for inviting him over, Rex being here feels like a thick, cool layer of salve on tonight's new wounds.

Rex interlocks his fingers with mine, presses his palms into mine, and brings our hands up to frame our faces.

I press back, hard, even harder, and he takes a step back. Ha! He wasn't ready for that.

"Oh, so first you want to ignore me and now you want to push me around," he says, grinning.

I keep pushing, and he keeps stepping backward until he's up against my bed and then lying back with his feet on the floor. "Sorry, I didn't have the best day," I say, standing between his legs.

"Yeah, I figured the doctor didn't give you the okay for the playoffs. I'm so sorry."

I wish. But sadly, that's not it. How can I tell him that I'm pissed about having to play? That I would be absolutely fine with never touching another basketball the rest of my life. It seems impossible.

And it's not exactly going to be easy telling him that Daddy is trying to use him to bribe me and Cole to leave our mother, either. I'm glad he's occupying himself with looking around at my walls while I come up with the right words.

He looks back up at me and says, "It's okay. You have next year. Senior year is what really counts."

"The doctor actually gave me the okay today," I blurt out, and all my secrets dart off to dark corners inside me, hoping they're not next. I lie down next to Rex on my bed and look at the ceiling, the only blank space in my room.

"Yeah?" he asks, and out of the corner of my eye, I see him turn his head toward me.

I stare straight ahead. I can't have this conversation looking into his eyes when all my secrets are being so shy. I grab his hand, trying to let my secrets know that Rex is okay. Then I take a deep breath and say, "Basketball is not why I had a bad day. I know I said that my parents were just taking a break, but they're not. They're getting a divorce. Like, there's no hope. It's really happening."

"So you can play?" Rex asks.

Not, *Sorry about your parents.*

Not, *Sorry about your family breaking apart.*

Not, *Are you okay?*

Not even, *So what's all this stuff on your walls?*

So you can play? That's all he has to say.

● REX ●

Carli snatches her hand away from mine and places it on her belly. "Can I play? Is that all you care about? I swear, everything with you is always about basketball."

Wait! What? Hand aching with abandonment, I answer, "No, of course not."

"Well, I sure as hell can't tell."

Hold up a second. Did Carli just curse at me? Cursing in general and cursing *at* somebody are two different things. But I tell myself to be cool and roll over on my side to face her, hoping she'll face me, too.

She gives me a hard glance before staring back up at the ceiling.

Be cool, Rex. Be cool. "I knew you were going to the doctor today. When I didn't hear back from you, I was worried that you were going to have to sit out the rest of the season. Can you blame me for that?"

No answer. She rolls her eyes and starts fiddling with her necklace without even bothering to look in my direction.

Be cool, Rex. Be cool. "I mean, I drove all the way over here just to make sure you were okay."

She glares at me, says, "Nobody asked you to come over here," and looks back at the ceiling.

Okay. Clearly I have Carli confused. And it's my fault. I've texted her sixteen times today. And called her three. And then brought my ass all the way over here in the freezing cold to check on her. But you see, I'm not that dude. That dude that's going to be sweating her. That dude she can ignore and treat however bad she wants. That dude she can push around. Clearly she thinks I'm that dude. But he is not I.

And I get it, her parents are breaking up. But it's kinda old news, isn't it? It's not like they just plopped it on her today like, *Surprise!* They're not even living together.

Don't get me wrong, I'm sure the whole situation is still sad. But if she didn't feel like talking (even after she got the great news from her doctor), she could've at least sent a text telling me she'd hit me up tomorrow or something. But no. Nothing. And now instead of apologizing, she wants to treat me like shit? Naw, dawg. I'm not even going out like that.

I sit up in the bed and look over at her, and she actually has the nerve to look up at me with an attitude. Like I'm the one in the wrong.

"Don't worry. I won't be poppin' up over your house again," I say.

"Good" is all she says and closes her eyes.

A hurt deep inside me hurls its voice up through a dark sky. "Good? Really, Carli?"

She ignores me.

Another hurt, another hurl, but my throat closes over its voice. *How could you do me like this? After everything we've shared. And now it's like I'm nothing to you. Like I'm nobody,* I scream inside myself.

I swallow my hurt back down. "It's getting late," I say, and stand up.

Cole walks in. "So, I was thinking," he says before he sees me. And then after, "Rex!" and gives me a giant hug. I don't think a hug has ever been more on time.

"Not now, Cole," Carli says, and sits up on the bed, face scrunched up.

Cole turns to me. "Did Carli tell you that we may be going to your—"

"Are you out of your fucking mind?" Carli screams, and stands up. "Out! Get out! Now!"

Hurt welling up in his eyes, he turns to walk out.

"What's going on in here?" their mom asks, appearing in the doorway behind him.

No one speaks. Everyone's looking at Carli. Her fists are balled up, her jaw is clenched, and her nostrils are flared like she wants to give us all a serious beatdown.

Part of me wants to go to her, hug her, and make her relax. But the other part, the part that's been working overtime my whole life to hold myself together, demands that I stay back.

THAT'S
ALL
SHE
WROTE

CARLI

Monday after school and I'm at basketball practice, where I'm supposed to be learning new defensive plays. But I can't stop running the scene of Rex leaving my room through my head. How he looked at me like he didn't know me. How I looked back at him, with all the anger I felt about my parents' divorce, their custody battle, basketball, my life. How Mom put her hand on his back and said, "I'll walk you out," and I let her, without even telling him good-bye.

"Jordan, if Shannon gets the ball at the top of the left key, go and help Carli trap her," Coach says, and points to the left corner of the free-throw line. Jordan walks down to the corner from right outside the three-point line, smacking on gum.

I haven't told Jordan about the breakup. Rex and I haven't officially said we were over, but what we had definitely feels broken. No more rise-and-shine texts from him every morning. No more staying up late talking to him on the phone every night. No contact at all since he left my house on Friday.

"Carli, get your head out of the clouds and come up here to trap!" Coach yells. The whole team's eyes widen in surprise. Jordan's mouth is literally hanging open.

Coach never yells at me. Everybody else, yes, but never me.

"Shannon cost us the championship last year, and I'll be damned if I let her take it away from us again this year," Coach continues.

Shannon is this sophomore from Langham High. Yeah, she can ball, but she ain't all that. Plus, she's always looking at me funny and trying to copy my style. Been on varsity since she was a freshman, like me. Tall, six-foot-one to be exact, like me. Okay, maybe she can't help either of those two things, but she wears number twenty-two. Now, everybody and their mama know that's my number. And one time she slipped me a note after a game that said, "Hey." *Hey?* Like, she couldn't have opened her mouth to say that? I swear I can't figure out if the girl likes me or wants to be me. But either way, I can't stand her.

"You good?" Jordan whispers after I get to the corner.

"Rex and I broke up," I whisper back.

"Okay," Coach says, "now if Shannon gets the ball on the right key, Carli, you drop back down to the block. Jordan, you slide over. And Meagan, you come up to help Jordan."

"Are you serious?" Jordan asks as we switch positions.

After practice Jordan and I go to Baskin-Robbins in Rice Village. Once we get our ice cream, we sit outside at a hot pink bistro table, backs against the red brick building. It's eighty degrees. Houston sure knows how to flip the switch on the weather, but nobody's mad at it today. Everybody and their mama are out walking and shopping and eating in the sun.

Cold sweetness dissolving on my tongue, I explain, "It would be everything spending senior year with Rex, but leave my mom? I can't do that." Oh, I had to tell Jordan about the whole thing with my parents because the whole thing with Rex wouldn't make any sense otherwise. Plus, I'm tired of keeping so many secrets.

"Not only that, you can't leave the team your senior

year! It's crazy your dad is even asking you to. What is he thinking?" Jordan asks, and tucks in her outstretched legs to make room for a woman walking by on the sidewalk with a stroller.

I'm leaving the team either way, I think but don't dare say. Jordan will never forgive me. Like, our friendship will be over. I stay silent and scoop out another spoonful of my Cannoli Be With You ice cream—mascarpone, pistachios, crunchy cannoli shell pieces, and chocolate chips. Some goodness I need right about now.

"So, you think you'll be ready for Shannon?" Jordan asks, and eats a scoop of her Pink Bubblegum ice cream with sprinkles, chocolate chips, Butterfinger pieces, and cherries. Leave it up to Jordan to mess up ice cream.

"I guess," is all I say, hoping she'll drop the basketball talk.

"She gave us some serious problems last year, and that's when she was a freshman. No telling what she's gonna be coming with this year."

When Jordan says *us*, she means me. Shannon plays *my* position. *I'm* the one who has to guard her. And I'm not sure how I'm supposed to do that when I don't even want to play.

"I need to say something to Rex," I say, trying to change the subject. "But I don't know what."

"*I'm sorry* sounds like it will do just fine."

"But what about the fact that all he wanted to do was talk about basketball even after I told him about my parents?" I don't know why I just bothered to ask Jordan that. It's all she ever wants to talk about, too.

"Well, you didn't even tell him the real deal. It's not like he knows you and Cole have to decide which parent to live with. He's not a mind reader, Carli. Plus, it *is* a big deal that you'll be back for the playoffs. No way we could handle Shannon without you."

"Couldn't handle her with me. So, what's the difference?"

"Girl, stop. You are Carli Alexander and you are about to shut Shannon down," she says, and reaches her spoon for my bowl. I swear Jordan's always trying to steal somebody's food.

I move my bowl over and shield it with my hand. "Eww, I don't want all that nastiness mixed up with all this goodness."

She sucks her spoon clean and tries again.

Disgusting, but I let her. Hoping that she'll remember this. Hoping that this will somehow count when I have to tell her the truth about basketball.

● REX ●

I'm running down the court, trying to get back on D, when I spot them. Light-blue scrubs walking up the stands. A tall, slim man with dark skin and a low-cut fade. Halfway up, the man in scrubs sits down, and I see his face. My father. For the first time ever, my father is at my game.

The dude I'm supposed to be guarding shoots a three. *Swish.*

Shit.

"Take that, Mr. Rex Carrington," dude says, shooting hand still hanging in the air. He's wearing yellow wristbands on both wrists to match his uniform.

"Man, get on somewhere. That's your first three the whole game," I reply, and give him a light bump while running back up the court.

The ref blows her whistle and a jolt of fear rushes through my body. *Not another technical!* But she holds up her hand to signal a time-out.

"Hustle up! Hustle up!" Coach Bell shouts, waving his right arm in a big circle. As I approach the huddle, he gives me a water bottle and asks, "You all right? You didn't even have a hand in his face."

"I'm good. I'm good." I take the water bottle, hold it up, and squeeze, giving myself the cold smack in the face I need. When I look back at my father, he's staring straight at me.

"Listen!" Coach Bell says, crouched down in the middle of the huddle. "We only have three minutes left and we're down six. We need everybody's head in the game right now." He looks up at me. "If we lose tonight, it's over. No going to San Antonio to play for the championship. And we've worked too hard and come too far for that. We can do this. We have to do this!" He stands up and puts his hand out. The whole team piles their hands on. "'Hustle hard' on three. One. Two. Three."

"Hustle hard!" And we lift our hands and run back to our positions.

Danny brings the ball up the court and passes to me just outside the three-point line on the left.

Dude guarding me is moving back and forth with his hands outstretched and his sweaty brown hair stuck to his forehead, saying, "Whatchu got? Whatchu got?"

Does this cornball really think he can hold me? He probably does because my shot has been off all night. But that has nothing to do with him. I've been thinking about Carli. I swear that girl is always throwing me off my game some kind of way. I pass it back to Danny, and he swings it around to our shooting guard, Tommy.

Tommy gives his defender a little head fake, dribbles past him, and passes the ball to Josh at the top of the key. Coach has been playing us both lately when he wants to go with more of a small-ball lineup.

Next thing you know, Josh is passing the ball to me. Wasn't expecting that! And neither was dude guarding me. I gather my legs underneath me and release, feeling my father watching me.

Swish!

The crowd erupts in cheers, and my father is on his feet, clapping. And I swear each time his hands come together, I hear a thousand claps. All the claps from all the games he's ever missed. Every *Good job, son* or *I'm so proud of you* that I've always wanted to hear. And I'm taking all of it in.

"Let's go!" I yell, slap the court with both hands, and sprint to get back on defense.

Danny swipes the ball off the other team's point guard. And I'm running full speed back toward our basket. Corny dude is running alongside me, but he can't stop what's about to go down. As I approach the basket, I leap, catch Danny's perfectly thrown alley-oop, and do a 360 midair before *boom*—that's all she wrote!

The whole gym goes crazy, and the other team calls a time-out. We're still one point down, but the momentum has already shifted in our direction. Ain't no way we're about to let these fools beat us now.

CARLI

Clearly Rex isn't feeling my *I'm sorry.* Texted him over three hours ago and still haven't heard back. Now I'm in my room, sitting at my desk, making him a card. The first card I've ever made for anybody. Hopefully something he can feel.

The front has no words. Only our bodies from that picture Cole took of us sitting on Daddy's swallow-you-whole sofa. It's not a great picture of me—mostly hair with a little bit of profile looking at Rex.

But Rex's face is everything. In it, I can feel what he sees in me. I swear it's like walking to the center of his heart and seeing my own reflection. A bright, glorious, confident girl. Nothing like how I see myself.

I cut us away from the background and paste us on

gold linen card stock. Then I break out all the LePens I own and draw a big, swirly sun behind us. Arrange a coral peony cut from a magazine to look like I'm handing it to him. And paste four tissue-papered lavender rays straight from my heart to his. Hoping he'll feel how sorry I am. Hoping he'll feel what I see in him. A fiercely tender boy. A million streaks of softness, cutting through all the dark clouds.

I push down the peony, smoothing the thin, glossy paper over the glue. The card actually looks pretty cool. Better than most of the cards in Mom's shop, I'll tell you that.

"I've decided," Cole says, walking into my room. Didn't need to break out an *I'm sorry* for Cole. Friday night seemed to slip right off him.

"Please tell me the blue one," I say, turning around in my chair. He was in here five minutes ago holding up a basic blue T-shirt and a red silky shirt that looked like it came straight out of a nineties R&B video, asking which one he should wear on his date. After school tomorrow he's taking this senior from his photography class to the Cockrell Butterfly Center. Or I should say, she's taking him. She's the one with a license, so she'll be picking him up.

"No, I mean I'm going to live with Dad next year."

"What!" I stand up from my chair so fast that it nearly falls over. "I thought we said we'd decide together?"

"Shh. Can you be any louder? Mom is home." He extends his long arm and pushes the door to my bedroom closed.

"Yeah, and you want to leave her, your own mom, just so you can go to school with Rex," I whisper hard, and walk away from him to my bed.

After I sit down, I glimpse Cole's pink ice cream cone–patterned socks, and an image of the light pink house shoe in the middle of the road on the way to school this morning pops in my head. It was on the white separating line, still fresh and fluffy, like it hadn't been run over yet. At the time I took it as a sign that me and Rex still had a chance.

But now I'm thinking the abandoned house shoe was trying to tell me not to leave Mom. Even in its fresh fluffiness, it still looked forgotten and sad. How could I even think about leaving Mom alone like that? Not that I planned to. But I'd be lying if I said I haven't imagined spending my last year with Rex—kissing between classes, walking down the hall holding hands, throwing our caps in the air together on the day the rest of our lives begin.

"No, Woodside High has a better boys' basketball program and one of the best photography teachers in the state," Cole says, and walks over to sit beside me. "She's always doing celebrity portraits for *Texas Monthly* and food photography for *PaperCity Magazine* and *Houston Press*. She even has credits in *National Geographic* and *Travel and Leisure*." He looks around at my walls. "There may even be something of hers in here."

"Oh, my bad. So, it's Rex, basketball, and a teacher you don't even know you'll have over Mom," I say, and scoot away from him, trying to make myself feel superior for only thinking of leaving Mom and never saying it aloud.

"Look, it's not like Dad can stop me from seeing Mom. I'll see her whenever I want. I could go by her shop or stop over for dinner or come spend weekends with y'all whenever. We're not little kids anymore, Carli. Our parents are still our parents, yeah, but they can't control us like they used to."

"What are you talking about?" I say, and stand up. "Of course they can control us! Didn't you hear Daddy? He's filing for sole custody!"

"I'm almost positive Dad was just pissed when he said all that stuff. Divorce gets ugly like that," he says in a calm voice, grabs my hand, and tries to get me to sit back down.

I snatch my hand away. "Oh, you're such the adult. You have all the fucking answers."

Cole doesn't reply. He looks up like he's surprised by me. Then like he's sorry for me and disappointed in me.

I don't know who he thinks he is, looking at me like that. He's the one talking about leaving Mom on the side of the road. I should be the one giving him the disappointed looks. But I can barely meet his eyes.

He's still looking at me, but his face isn't saying anything anymore. It's just as silent as his mouth.

I can't take this silence. The stillness of it. The way it's making me look back at this messed-up, pissed-off girl who has no problem pushing her own brother away. Not to mention the first boy who's ever given her a glimpse of a higher version of herself. I can't stand her right now.

"Sorry," I say, and sit back down. The apology is meant for tonight and Friday, but I don't say all that.

Pretty sure Cole gets it, though, because he puts his arm around me. "I still want us to stick together, I do. I just thought you should know where I stand. After this year you'll only have one year of high school left, but I'll have two. It's a bigger decision for me."

Is this boy really trying to minimize the impact this decision is going to have on my life? But I stay cuddled up under his arm, tell myself to calm down. "I'm not saying I won't go live with Daddy, but we still have two weeks. Let's use our time to think it all through."

"You're right . . . we should," Cole says, and squeezes me.

"And promise we'll talk about this again before we make our final decision, before you tell anyone?"

"Promise," he says. "This stays between us."

REX

There's no reason I should still be awake. It's after midnight, and I'm lying in bed with the lights out. The house is wonderfully warm. My belly is comfortably full. And the frame, the entrance to the hall that leads to my father's room, got a great picture tonight.

After my father and I ate Thai takeout and watched a

little late-night TV, he filled up the frame for over an hour, talking about my game.

We won, just like I thought. And I hit the winning shot—a three from the baseline. The whole team tackled me in joy. Josh even rubbed my head. And Danny actually texted me tonight after the 360 alley-oop dunk made ESPN's high school highlight reel. I should be sleeping like a baby.

But I can't stop thinking about Carli. About that text she sent—*Sorry*. That's it. No elaboration. What am I supposed to say back to that? *It's okay?* No, because it's not. *I forgive you?* No, because I don't. I need more words. An explanation of why she was acting like that. A promise to never treat me that way again.

My phone lights up and I quickly grab it off my nightstand. Another text from Carli saying the same thing:

Sorry

I don't respond.

The next day, fourth period, honors chemistry: **I'm sorry**

Oooo, she added the word *I'm*. All the words that usually roll off her tongue and this is the best she can come up with? I don't respond.

Wednesday after basketball practice, grabbing my

precalculus book out of my locker to take home:

I

M

S

O

R

R

Y

She's getting a little creative with it. Won't lie, makes me smile, but I don't respond. You see, she ignored sixteen of my texts last Friday and three of my calls (yep, I still remember). I've only ignored one-fourth that amount, and she hasn't even bothered to call. I have to make it to eight, so she at least knows half of how I felt. Yes, petty, but sometimes it beez like that.

Thursday, at 6:47 a.m., same time I used to give her a wake-up text: **I'm sorry, Rex**

Damn, she gets me with this one. I know it's only one added word, but it's my name and I can hear her saying it. I type, **I'm sorry too . . . for ignoring you. I miss you**. But I decide that once again I'm doing way too much and erase everything.

After school on Friday: **What's your address? I have something to send you**

I wonder what it is. Did she buy me an apology present?

Maybe some new Js. Did she make a donation to plant some trees in my name? Yo, what if she wrote me a poem and kissed it with glossy lips? Hahaha, I'm being stupid. But really, what if she did? I want to ask her. I want to joke and play with her. I want to talk to her and see her and hug her and kiss her.

But this is only her sixth text. So, I only respond with my address—no *hello* or *how are you doing*. She better be glad I'm even texting her back.

SECRET
SPOTS

CARLI

Nineteen East Shady Trail is this huge, white, futuristic house surrounded by a pine forest. It has a sloped roof that juts out from the rest of the house, toward the sky, and is perched on concrete piers. As I walk up the steel staircase on the side of the house that leads to the front door, trying to think of the words that will make Rex forgive me, it feels like I'm boarding a giant spaceship. Like maybe, just maybe, Rex will open the door and we'll blast off to the stars, leaving all our earthly problems behind.

● REX ●

I open the door and it's Carli. At my house. Standing on my porch. Wearing some button-fly cutoffs and a vintage *Jaws* T-shirt. In front of the setting sun. Damn, she couldn't be more perfect. So perfect I have to stop myself from picking her up, twirling her around, and carrying her into the house— honeymoon style.

Yeah, Rex. Forget about how she ignored you. How bad she treated you when you drove all the way over to her house in the freezing cold. And that look she gave you. Dawg, it was like she didn't give a shit about you. Yeah, go ahead and let all that slide.

"Look who's the stalker now," I say playfully. I mean, somebody had to say something. The silence was getting weird.

"No, you gave me your address."

"You said you were sending me something," I say. "Not coming over."

"Well, I lied!" Carli says, tilting her head and widening her eyes.

We both crack up laughing.

Call me a sucker, but damn being mad. I grab her hands, pull her into the house, and tell her, "I've missed you so much."

Carli closes her eyes, almost like it hurts, and puts her head down. She looks like she's about to cry. I pull her into me, and she buries her face in my shoulder. Warm tears soak through my T-shirt and she's shaking.

What the hell just happened? I'm so confused. She was just laughing. *Wait, did I do this? I swear to God I hate myself for ignoring her like that.*

"I'm sorry," I say softly. "I'm so, so sorry," I repeat, holding her tight and rubbing her back in slow circles, the way Angie used to rub mine as a child.

CARLI

"There's so much I need to tell you," I say under my breath, voice squeaking and trembling all over the place. I don't expect him to understand me. I mean, I can barely understand myself. One minute I'm acting like a raging lunatic, the next minute I'm laughing up a storm, and the next I'm crying uncontrollably. I swear I don't know who I am anymore.

"You can tell me anything. You know that, right?" Rex

says, separates from me a little, and kisses my forehead with soft, wet lips. "I want you to tell me . . . everything. I want to know all of you."

I don't lift my head. Thick mucus is running down the slope below my nose and hanging over my top lip. *Can you say gross?* Oh, my gosh; I got it all over the shoulder of his white T-shirt.

"I have a lot to tell you, too," he says, lifts my chin, and looks me in the eyes.

I quickly turn my head to wipe the snot on my shoulder. And now it's smeared all over my right cheek. *Great, just great.* But it's weird . . . I don't feel embarrassed. The fact that Rex can see me like this and not run away . . . see me like this and still look at me like I'm his everything makes me feel safe . . . and free . . . like I'm home.

"There's snot all over your shirt," I say.

"Yeah, it's all over your cheek, too."

"I know. I can feel it crusting up on my skin."

"Damn, you nasty," Rex says, and gives me a smack on the lips. The kiss is quick, but his lips do indeed touch mine. Yes, where the snot just was. This boy must be into me, like, for-real-for-real.

● REX ●

After a quick stop in the bathroom, I give Carli a tour of the house. Trust, not my idea. But she seems to really be into its design. She's talking about its clean lines . . . its floor-to-ceiling windows . . . its lack of trim around the doors . . . its sloped ceiling . . . its linear air vents . . . its unadorned walls . . . its minimalism this . . . and modern that . . . and on and on and on.

"I'm glad you like it, but I sure as hell don't," I tell her, walking up the stairs.

"Seriously? How could you not? Look at it. There's so much empty space. Even these floating stairs. I mean, it's everywhere. I don't know . . . it makes me feel light and airy. Free in a way."

"You get all of that from a whole bunch of blank walls and hard-ass furniture?" I ask, stepping off the top step and heading to my room.

"I guess my house is the exact opposite. There's stuff everywhere you look. And you've seen my room, my walls. Looking at so much stuff can get exhausting. Don't get me wrong; I love my mom's decorating style and I love everything I put up on my walls. But right now my mind feels so full. I'm just saying some emptiness would be nice."

I open the door to my room. "Well, you're not about to get it in here."

CARLI

Rex wasn't kidding. Everywhere I look there's something new for my eyes to land on. Other than the wall straight ahead with the sliding-glass door leading outside, there's stuff everywhere.

"I'll grab us some snot-free tees," Rex says, and laughs.

"You're never going to let me forget about that, are you?"

"Nope," he says, and disappears into his walk-in closet to the left.

"I can't wait until you slip up and do something embarrassing," I say loudly, walking toward the wall-to-wall shelving unit to the right.

"Yeah, yeah, yeah."

On the top shelf, there's a display box with a collection of pinned beetles between an old encyclopedia set and a framed pencil sketch of someone hugging a huge tree. On the shelves below, there are two globes, various art history books, a record player, a big stack of records, four African female busts wearing Rex's baseball caps, a small green lamp sitting on a gold tray, and a ceramic red-and-blue clock. On his nightstand there's a miniature rocking chair holding a silver watch on a stack of worn novels.

"Who knew you had such eclectic taste? I like . . . I like," I say.

"Huh?" Rex shouts from the closet.

"Oh, nothing," I mumble under my breath and walk over to his desk in the corner near his closet. His desk is actually an old wooden drafting table with a brass-and-steel file cabinet underneath it for drawers. On it there's a silver vintage pencil sharpener and five neatly sharpened number-two pencils beside an opened precalculus book. *Dang, this boy loves him some math.* Above his desk there's a roughly sketched portrait of a woman with two french braids.

I want to ask, *Is that your mom?* But I'm not ready to feel anymore sadness. Instead, I divert my eyes to the glass dome paperweight sitting on the upper right corner of his desk on top of a small notepad from Hotel Locarno Roma.

"Cool! You and your dad have been to Rome?" I shout, picking up the paperweight. There's an abstract purple-and-blue watercolor painting inside.

Rex's muffled voice comes from the closet. "Ha! Real funny. I seriously have so much to tell you."

I'm tired of shouting. So I put the paperweight down and follow his voice into the closet, where he's bent over looking inside his bottom built-in drawer along the left wall. When he sees me, he stands up with a shirt in his hand.

But there's not one on his body.

REX

Carli is looking at me like I'm a straight-up snack. Like if she could, she would fold me in half, slap some peanut butter on me, and chomp away. I'm not gon' even lie, she has your boy feeling a little shy up in here. I bite my lip to ease the embarrassment.

CARLI

Oh my goodness. He did not just bite his bottom lip. Is he trying to make me lose my mind? In this small space with his smooth, brown skin . . . his hard chest . . . his six-pack. And don't even let me get me started on his dips. You know those creases that start at his hips and angle down toward his . . .

REX

"This is the smallest shirt I could find," I say, trying to take some of the attention off me, and hold out a long-sleeved black-and-navy striped tee.

CARLI

Did he just invite me to come closer? Is that what he did? Okay, if he says so.

The first thing I do when I get to him is rub my hands down his chest and abs—hard and moisturized. I usually behave a little better than that, but I can't help myself.

Then I start taking off my shirt. I mean, I'm looking at

him so it's only fair for him to be looking at me, right?

Rex must agree because he's helping me get it over my shoulders and head.

He grabs my bare waist with both hands and I swear . . .

REX

If I could run off into my future with Carli right now, I would. No lie. But for now, I pull her body into mine. We're so close I can see the faint tear streaks on her cheeks, so close I can feel her heat. Like it's seeping into my chest, taking over me.

I gently dig my fingers into her waist, and she parts her mouth and reaches her lips toward mine. Her lip over my bottom lip, her tongue over my tongue, her breath mixing with my breath. Soft and wet. And hard.

CARLI

I'm feeling Rex like I've never felt another boy, and I want to feel more. I press into him and kiss him harder. Faster. It's like my mouth, my body, can't get enough.

His hands are underneath my ribs and I'm up on the dresser.

My lips race toward the closest part of his face, his forehead, and then down to the mole on the side of his nose, back to his mouth. My hands wrap around his neck, and his travel up over my bra.

He pulls away, his big black eyes asking me if it's okay.

Yes! And I let out a moan as his fingers touch the tips of my nipples. Again as his wet tongue moves in circles, as his mouth sucks.

His hands on my thighs. His fingers up the outsides of my jean shorts.

But I want them on the inside.

● REX ●

Carli's moving her waist in circles. Somebody, help. Please. We cannot have sex in this closet. Don't get me wrong, we could very well have sex in this closet. Dude, if we don't stop with all this kissing and touching and circling, we will definitely have sex in this closet. And it would be amazing. I've waited forever and a day to make love. But I don't have condoms. And what I wouldn't love is having a baby right now.

 CARLI

Rex takes his mouth off me and slides his hands down to my knees.

"Will your dad be home soon?" I ask.

"Nah, he'll probably be at the hospital all night," he says, and brings one of his hands back up. I will it to my breasts, but he reaches higher and runs his fingers along my collarbone underneath my thin, gold chain. Balancing my medallion on his middle finger, he says, "I've never really taken a good look at this before. It's dope."

"Thanks," I say, lean down, and grab his bottom lips with my lips.

He pulls away. "I don't have any condoms."

"Oh," I say, feeling heat start to escape. There's nothing sexy about the thought of getting pregnant right now. I might not know what I want to do with my life, but I do know I want options.

He hands me his shirt and I put it on. It smells like him, a mixture of pine trees and sweat. "You must've not washed this after you wore it last."

"Don't know. Here, you want another one?" he asks, bending down to look in his drawer.

"No, I love the way your funk smells."

"Okay, you're officially nasty," he says, laughing, and slides on a black long-sleeved T-shirt.

"And you love it."

REX

Back in my room, I'm sitting on my bed and Carli is walking

around looking at everything. Touching everything. She picks up a small gold-and-pearl turtle off my nightstand and lifts its shell. "Where do you get all this stuff?" she asks. "Do you go antiquing?"

"Antiquing? Man, nah. I found it all in some boxes marked for donation during our move. It all belonged to my mom."

She can't put down the turtle fast enough. "Why would your dad want to give your mom's stuff away? It's all so cool."

"I don't know. When we moved, it seemed like he wanted to leave everything behind, including my mom." The words feel so right coming out. Like they needed to be said. They've been floating around in my head since we moved out here last summer.

"Your dad doesn't care that you kept it all and have it up here?"

"He doesn't know."

"What do you mean he doesn't know?"

"Well, he's never been up here. So—"

"Wait. Your dad has never been in your room?"

"I told you I had a lot to tell you."

Carli's standing beside my bed with her hands clasped in front of her—hush-mouthed. She clearly doesn't know what to say about my father. And she hasn't picked up anything else. Don't know if she thinks I would care or Mom would care, but either way, it's starting to feel way too heavy in here. "I have something I want to show you," I say, get up, and grab my backpack from the corner beside the sliding door. "Come on."

CARLI

Rex is leading me across his backyard by the hand. When the lawn ends and the forest begins, he doesn't pause. But it's dark. And who knows what's in there.

I stop. "Umm, where are we going?" I ask, and fold my arms across my chest like it's cold, even though it's pretty warm.

"Come on. You'll see. Trust me."

I don't move. I feel like I'm the star of a scary movie and the audience is screaming, *Girl, don't do it.*

"I come back here all the time. You'll love it," he promises.

The audience is still screaming, *Don't listen to him, girl. Not unless you want to die!* And to their point, what good can come out of walking into a dark forest at night?

Rex reaches into his backpack, takes out a big flashlight,

and shines it into the woods. "See, just trees." He lights the ground. "And dead leaves and shrubs and fungus. No boogeyman."

"What about snakes and raccoons and whatever else lives in there."

"We'll be fine," Rex says, and shines the light at our feet.

In protest, I take a deep breath and let it out slow and loud. But when he grabs my hand, I start walking again.

After a few minutes, we reach a clearing with a wooden picnic table. "You brought this out here?" I ask.

"Yeah, it used to be in the backyard at my old house," he says, and takes out a long, red lighter, like Daddy uses to light the barbeque pit. He hands me the flashlight and lights two tin citronella candles sitting on the benches, one on each side of the table. Then he takes a blanket out of his backpack and arranges it on top of the picnic table.

"This is actually pretty cool," I say, admiring the setup.

"You better listen to your boy," Rex says, smiling, and climbs up on the table.

I climb up, too.

And now we're lying on top of the table with our pinky fingers linked, looking up at the crowns of tall pines reaching for a patch of star-sprinkled sky.

REX

This has always been my secret spot. Even at my old house, when there was just a tiny backyard with two cedar elm trees. This table, the trees, the stars, this stillness—they've always been there for me. And now Carli is here, and it's like I've introduced her to my best friends and they're vibin'. And it's making me feel closer to her than I've ever felt. Like even if we were butt-naked having sex, I doubt I'd feel closer.

"Crazy that there are more trees on Earth than stars in the Milky Way, isn't it?" Carli says, her voice soft beside me.

I was already looking up at the stars, but I look closer. At all the bright spots peeking out from the darkness. At the giant pines stretching toward them. "Are there really?" I ask, wondering why I've never come across that fact.

"Yeah, there's something like three trillion trees on the planet. But scientists estimate there are somewhere between one hundred and four hundred billion stars in the galaxy."

"Word? I never would've guessed that. Especially since fifteen billion trees are chopped down every year. Did you know that almost fifty percent of the trees on the planet have either been cut down or died some kind of way since humans have been around?" I ask, offering up my own facts.

"Really? I knew all the Amazon boxes had to come from somewhere, but fifteen billion? Dang, at this rate, our stars are going to start catching up to our trees."

"I know, right?" I say, feeling my insides grin because I'm sitting in my favorite place talking to my favorite person about one of my favorite things. I didn't even think Carli was into trees like that. She acted like she barely cared about the magnolia dying outside of her dad's house. "Who knew you were into trees?"

"I'm not," she says, bursting my little bubble.

"So, you're into stars then?"

"Well, kinda. But I'm more into random facts. I like collecting ones I find interesting and putting them up on my walls."

"Yeah, I saw all the stuff in your room. It's dope. You must not let Cole take pictures in there because I've never seen your walls on his feed."

"Cole and his Instagram," she says, like she's rolling her eyes. "Yeah, no pictures of my walls allowed."

"Why not?"

"Magic?"

"Yeah, I've always found magic in small, random things . . . in thinking about them . . . in piecing them together . . . in seeing what they may have to say about big, important things."

"What do they say?"

"A lot. But nothing, really. I don't know. I mean, my walls still have a lot to tell me. And I can't have them out there speaking to everyone else before they even let me know what's up," she says, and laughs a little.

I love talking to Carli like this. It's like I'm inside her mind, hearing how it works. "So what are you waiting on them to tell you?" I ask.

"Everything," she says.

"Everything like what?" I ask, remembering her necklace. It looked magical. I sit up on my elbow and reach for it. Rub my thumb along the curved left edge, where the raised crescent moon sits cradling a sun in the form of a cut-out circle. From the circle I slide my thumb along the engraved rays that reach toward tiny raised stars on the other side. It's like she has the whole universe dangling from her neck.

"I don't know. Just everything."

"Everything is a lot."

"I know."

It feels like she's kicked me out of her mind. I want back in, but I don't know which words will get me there. So I lie back down. Don't say anything.

And neither does she.

For a long minute.

Then she shifts around on the table. "I can't see you," she whispers. Her words—after our long, dark silence— feel like a spark.

I roll on my side to face her like she's facing me. "I can't see you, either," I say into the blackness. There's only a sliver of a moon tonight. And I'm not sure when, but our candles went out.

"But I'm here," she responds.

It's weird. In the darkness, it's almost like we don't have bodies. Like we're spirits in the night. "You know I come out here to feel closer to my mom," I say, imagining Mom's spirit floating around us through the trees.

"I can see that. Out here, it's like we're closer to God or the Universe or whatever you want to call the mystery of all there is. And I guess your mom is a part of all that now."

"Yeah, I guess she is," I say, thinking about Mom's soul leaving the Earth, traveling out of our solar system, out of our galaxy, and on and on through the stars forever.

Carli puts the palm of her hand against my chest.

"My father blames me for her death, you know," I say, surprised at how easy the words glide out of my mouth. "I mean, he's never said it, but he's pretty much ignored me my whole life. And I always knew why. Then he went off and sold our old house. The house my mom lived in, my biggest connection to her, without even telling me first."

"Oh my gosh. That's awful. I'm so sorry," she says.

"It's okay. We're cool, now," I try to reassure her. "Actually, you know that video your dad made?"

"Yeah."

"Well, I sent it to my father, and afterward he came to my game. Like, for the first time in my life. And we've been talking more. And he's been out of his room more. He used to stay in there all the time when he was home. I rarely saw him. But now we've even chilled on the sofa a few times. Oh, I forgot to tell you. We want to hire your mom to help us make the house more of a home."

"Wait . . . wait," Carli says. "You mean your father basically ignored you your whole life and sold your mom's old house, but now, just like that, everything is cool?"

In the darkness, her words almost feel like my own. The ones I've been shoving back down inside myself every time they try to rise up. But out here, I can't push them around. "No. I mean, it's surface cool, but that's it. We haven't really talked or gotten deep about anything, yet. And to be honest, I'm kind of afraid to. Afraid of everything that might come up. You don't even want to know. Let's just say I've felt a lot of bad things over the years."

"I'm sure you have." Her hand leaves my chest, and I feel its warm softness on my cheek.

We lie in silence for a minute, and I imagine her feeling everything I've felt—the confusion, the loneliness, the disappointment, the sadness, the hurt, the rage.

"Thanks for sharing all this with me," she says. "This place. All the stuff about your dad. I know it can't be easy to talk about."

"But it kinda is with you," I say. "Especially out here. I don't know. I wasn't lying when I said I'm trying to share everything with you. You saw what happened when we were keeping things to ourselves. I was trying to act all hard and not answer your calls, but that shit sucked ass!"

She laughs. "That's what you get for ignoring me."

"What about you ignoring me? What was that about?"

Carli removes her hand from my cheek and goes quiet.

"No more secrets," I say.

"No more secrets," she repeats.

"Nah, don't say it if you don't mean it."

"No, I do . . . I promise. On everything."

"I hate basketball," I say, feeling a huge swell of relief.

"I know it's gotta be hard," Rex says, and his hand—cool—finds my waist underneath his T-shirt.

Okay, I'm 200 percent sure that he's not taking me seriously. "I'm not speaking in hyperbole, here. I, Carli Alexander, can't stand basketball. Like, if you put one in front of me right now, I'd find something to stab it with. And as it deflated, I'd have a huge smile on my face. I'm grinning just thinking about it."

Crickets. The calls of two birds.

Rex laughs that awkward I-don't-get-the-joke laugh and gently squeezes my waist. "Sorry, what? I'm confused. I thought you loved basketball. You're a beast."

"Well, you thought wrong. There's a difference between being good at something and actually liking it. I'm only good because my dad has been coaching me since birth. I haven't been able to stand basketball since middle school."

"Middle school? Damn, so you're telling me that you've hated basketball the whole time you've been in high school?"

"Yep."

"Even the times you made the All-American team?"

"Yep."

"Even when y'all won the championship?"

"Yep."

"Even with—"

"Yes. The answer is gonna be *yes*," I say, getting a little annoyed.

"Sorry," he says, his voice going soft. "It's just hard to believe. If you've hated it for so long, why haven't you just quit?"

"It's not like I have anything better to do," I say, feeling myself sulk like a six-year-old who just got put in time-out.

"What do mean? You're interested in plenty of things."

"Yeah, but I don't have anything big to focus on."

"Big?"

"Yeah, like a . . . a," I say, the last word out of reach. It's always felt so much greater than me, so far away. And lately it's been worse, like it's running from me as fast as it can. Like maybe I'll never catch it.

Rex gently squeezes my waist, bringing me back into my body. And the shadowy trees behind him, the soft stream of light falling on their crowns, their limbs, the calls of invisible birds and insects, all seem to be telling me I'm wrong.

"A dream," I say, feeling some of my panic around the word soften.

"So. At least if you're doing something you like, you'd be getting closer to it. Don't get me wrong, it blows my mind that you don't want to ball. You're so damn good. But if you don't love it, you don't love it. Life is too short not to do what you love. Or at least what you like until you find what you love."

"You say that like it's easy. Like it would be cake to stop playing basketball and disappoint everyone I know. Well, besides my mom. She knows I hate basketball. But nobody else does. Not even Jordan, my best friend. She's our point guard. If we both win our games this week, you'll meet her at the championship next weekend."

"Wait. So, you're gonna play?"

"Yeah, started back playing this week. Figure the playoffs is not the best time to spring the news on my team. I'm going to tell them this summer."

More crickets and birds. Guess he's processing. And rubbing my ribs with his thumb. He can process all he wants as long as he keeps doing that.

"Wanna know another secret?" I ask, done with talking about basketball.

"You know I do."

"The very first kisses were blown in Mesopotamia as

a way to get in good with the gods."

"Huh?"

"Remember that secret I didn't tell you when we were sitting up in the stands after my surgery and you started getting mad?"

"I wasn't getting mad."

"Yes, you were. But anyway, when you blew a kiss that day on the court, the fact popped in my head."

"Wait, what is it again?"

"The very first kisses were blown in Mesopotamia as a way to get in good with the gods."

His thumb goes still on my ribs. "Where'd that come from?"

"I put it up on my wall after this boy blew me a kiss in, like, the fifth grade. The next day he tried to front like he blew it to somebody else, but I left the fact up there anyway. Didn't really think about it again until you blew me that kiss on the court. Well, at least blew it in my direction.

"Then the fact about kisses came rushing back to me, which I took as a sign that we were totally meant to be. So much so that while I was in the hospital that night, I rewrote the fact on the back of my dinner menu—even though I had *no idea* how you felt about me—and I saved it to give to you. Carried it around in my back pocket for almost a week. But then . . . well, it's a long story. But the bottom line is: it got lost. I was waiting to tell you about it until I could give it to you in person, so it would be special. But it looks like that's not gonna happen, so there you go."

"No. I mean, what's the story behind the fact? How exactly did blowing kisses allow people to get in good with the gods?" Rex asks, totally ignoring my whole romantic story.

"I don't know. That's all I wrote down," I say, disappointed.

He repeats the fact four times, like he wants to remember it forever.

"Yep, that's it," I finally say.

"Crazy I've never heard of that. You know I blow a kiss every time I go to the free-throw line, right?"

"So I've heard."

"I blow them to my mom," he says.

And here I am worried about my stupid romantic story. "Really?" I say.

"Yeah, every time I blow a kiss, I ask her for forgiveness."

A heavy weight drops down on my chest, "Oh Rex," I say, and reach for his cheek again.

His hand leaves my waist and lands on my hand. Then he interlaces his fingers with mine and brings our hands down to rest in the space between us.

"No, no, it's cool. This is actually really good," he says

cheerfully. "You see, your fact means that my kisses have probably been working. It's like all that stuff we were talking about earlier with my mom being a part of Everything. If she's a part of Everything, that means I've been getting in good with her every time I blow a kiss. I don't know if she's forgiven me yet, but if I keep blowing kisses, she'll definitely have to forgive me one day."

His happiness is so sad, I don't know where to begin.

I want to tell him that he doesn't need to be forgiven, that it's not his fault. But I've already told him that, and I'm starting to think that even if I tell him again, and again and again, we'd only go around and around in the same circle.

I want to cry for him. But what good would that really do?

I want to ask him where the bottom of his pain is. Like how many kisses will he have to blow to know he's forgiven? But it's clear he doesn't know that.

I want to shake him, maybe slap him, tell him that he needs to move on. But I'm afraid of how he'd turn on me.

I don't know what to do. How can I be his everything when so much of it has nothing to do with me?

It feels terrible, but I decide there's not much I can do about his pain and try to get out from under it by changing the subject. "Oh, and another secret: Cole and I have to decide which parent we want to live with. In what? Like, a week and a half."

"What! That's nuts! You told me your parents were getting divorced, but you didn't tell me y'all had to decide who to live with."

"Yeah, it's complicated."

"So how's that even going to work? Like, where would y'all go to school?" he asks, a hint of hope in his eyes.

I wish my eyes hadn't adjusted to the dark so I wouldn't have had to see that. Maybe I could've told him the truth. I swear on a stack of a thousand notebooks I don't want to lie to him. But what am I supposed to say? *I have the option to spend senior year with you, but I'm probably gonna pass?* I glance away from him and say, "Staying put. Cole and I have already agreed that switching schools on top of everything else would be too much."

Rex pulls me close to him. "Well, at least you don't have to deal with that."

REX

Fuzzy hair on my face before I feel her lips.

CARLI

I kiss him a thousand times. Until I exhaust my guilt about ditching his pain. My guilt about lying. Until there is only me and Rex. And the urgent pleasure of our lips. And my insides turning colors. Brilliant colors.

REX

I open my eyes. Pull my lips away from hers. Push her hair back away from her face. My hands are shaking.

I need her to know what she's given me.

Shaking so bad it feels like I'm taking off.

What I've always wanted . . . my whole life.

Like I'm blasting through dark clouds.

More than anything else.

CARLI

"I love you, Rex," I tell him. And I feel his trembling hands go still on the crown of my head. See his tender face burst open. Hear a hundred tiny bells toll in my heart. No false alarms.

REX

"I love you, too," I say, looking at her, looking at me. Feeling her, feeling me. "So much. You don't even know."

I kiss her.

After a while she pulls away and stares at me.

She kisses me.

After a while I pull away and stare at her.

And it's like we're two trees secretly sharing nutrients underground, two stars orbiting around all the things there's no language for.

TWO
AND
TWO

 CARLI

It's official. Shannon wants to be me.

"Do you see this chick?" I ask Jordan. We're walking toward the middle of the Alamodome court for the jump ball. The whole first level of the arena is packed out. Forty-five thousand people, Cole told me before the start of the game, in San Antonio to see us ball.

"How could I not? Girl got issues," Jordan says, and ties her new twists—royal blue to match our uniforms—up in a ponytail.

"Yeah, *Single Black Female*–type issues," I say, catching a shot of Jordan and me above on the jumbotron.

"I don't know. Maybe she's doing it to mess with you."

"Mess with me?"

"Yeah, maybe this is her version of the Lance Stephenson ear-blowing move. It sure did mess up LeBron. Don't let her throw you off your game, Carli," Jordan says before lightly elbowing me and walking to her position on the other side of the circle.

I'm in the middle of the circle, under what feels like a million bright lights, facing Shannon—that forward from Langham who gave us problems last year. The one who wears my number, twenty-two. Yeah, her.

Home chick has decided to dye her hair the same color as mine. Not a fiery red or a burgundy red or a violet red, which could all pass as reasonable ways to switch it up from her old black hair. Oh no, she chose a born-with-it red. A brownish, golden red. Ain't too many black ginger girls in this world, and I guess she *just* so happened to decide to become one of us.

"I like your hair," I tell her.

"Thanks," she replies, and shyly smiles—the corners of her pale lips, almost the same color of her pale skin, barely curving up. She clearly doesn't get the intended sarcasm. I need her to get it, but now the ref is here about to toss up the ball.

"Okay, ladies. We all know what's on the line. But let's keep it clean. Good luck," the spiky-haired man says, and steadies the ball in his right palm.

I place my right foot down so that it almost touches the center court line and bend down, ready to leap. Shannon does the same. I give her the hardest look I can muster—eyes squinted, nostrils flared, upper lip raised up. But her face stays calm, like she's unfazed. So, when the ref makes the toss, I take it back to first grade and shout, "Copycat!"

When I tap the ball to Jordan, Shannon's hand is nowhere in sight.

After I land, the ref gives me a cautionary look, but doesn't blow his whistle.

"Let's go!" I shout, and run back to get on the block. Time to teach this Shannon girl that she could never be me. Not even the girl I no longer want to be.

● REX ●

Carli has been on fire the whole game. Jump shots, hook shots, bank shots—all dropping. She even had the nerve to drain two threes. Dang, and another one! I stand up and shout, "That's my girl! That's my girl right there!"

The rest of my team is looking at me like I'm lame, but

I don't give a damn. It's the fourth quarter, and Allen High is twelve points up. Carli is about to take home the state championship! And as soon as she wraps up her game, your boy is about to snatch his championship up, too. We're out here doing it like Jay-Z and Beyoncé!

Cole sits down beside me. He's been rotating between me, his dad, and his mom the whole game. We're all spread out in the arena behind Allen's bench. "Did you see that?" he asks.

"Hell yeah, I saw it! I mean, I knew your sister could ball but damn. Threes? I didn't know she could shoot like that."

"Oh yeah. Carli can do it all," Cole says. Then he stands up and joins the cheerleaders clapping their hands and chanting, "*D-E-F-E-N-S-E*, go defense!"

The girl Carli's guarding, also sporting number twenty-two, misses another turnaround jumper. Carli snags the rebound, makes an overhead throw to Jordan, and sprints up the court. Jordan passes it back to her near the basket. Another two points for Carli, and the other team calls a time-out with six minutes and twenty-one seconds on the clock.

"That's what I'm talking about!" Cole shouts before sitting back down.

Man, I love having Cole around. He stays coming with the good vibes. "You know you're like the little brother I never had," I say, and put my arm around him.

In total Cole-fashion, he gently bangs his right fist on his chest a few times. "Dude, you don't even know what that means to me. I've looked up to you since as long as I can remember. I seriously can't wait to ball with you next year. It's going to be a dream," he says excitedly. Then he leans forward, looks over to my team, and shouts, "Woodside High here I come!" None of them pay him attention.

Wait, I'm confused. How is he talking about coming to Woodside when Carli told me last week that they were staying at Allen? Did things change? And if so, why didn't she tell me?

Well, maybe something changed today. "Yeah, it's going to be sick," I say, fronting like I know what's up. Can't be out here looking like my girl doesn't keep me in the loop. "Me, you, and Carli at the same school? What! They ain't ready," I say, half believing the words coming out of my mouth.

"Oh, has Carli been talking about living with Dad, too?" Cole asks, looking surprised. "Awesome! She's been talking like she wants to stay with Mom and go to Allen. I thought I'd have to put in work to bring her around, but it looks like you beat me to it. Thanks, bro!"

I'm too stunned to bother correcting him.

The time-out buzzer sounds, and Cole is back on his feet. "If I don't catch you before your game, good luck! Not that you'll need it. I know you're about to stomp them Matthew Gaines boys."

"Thanks," I say through a thin, forced smile. I swear to God, I'm a complete fucking fool. Not because she's choosing to stay at her school instead of coming to mine. (That's a huge decision dealing with family stuff that's way bigger than me.) But because I believed there was no way she would she lie to me. After all we shared? No way. In my sacred place? No way. When she promised no more secrets on everything? Nah, man. But she fixed her lips to tell me a lie anyway.

 CARLI

After the time-out, I'm back in Shannon's ear. "Fine, if you wanna be my impersonator, go ahead." We're running up the court. I've been hitting her with copycat lines all game. I'll admit, they're getting kind of stale. But hey, if it ain't broke. . . .

"I'm not trying to be you," Shannon responds, breathing heavily, and gets in position on the block. It's the first time she's responded the whole game.

Standing behind her, I give her a little shove in the back to let her know how much of a liar I think she is. Nothing the refs will notice, though.

She whips her head around, glares at me, and then calls for the ball. The two guard with the brown bob whips her a chest pass, and Shannon turns to face me.

"Oh, look. It's me on me," I say.

She pulls up to shoot, and I'm off my feet ready to block, ready to knock her shot into next week.

But she doesn't shoot. And I'm still in the air. And now she's around me scoring an easy two. *Damn.*

"I've had red hair all my life," Shannon says, catching the ball after it falls through the net. "I only started dying it black when I started playing you." She shoves the ball into my solar plexus on the sly.

All my breath rushes out at once. Everything in me wants to bend over, to wrap itself around the hurt. But I stay upright and pass the ball to the ref. "Why you so worried about me?" I manage to push out in a normal voice.

"You really don't know, do you?"

I take off running up the court and she runs right beside

me. Like, literally her shoulder touching my shoulder. "I know you have an obsession with me. That's what I know." Jordan holds up a four, and I run to the free-throw line. She passes me a quick overhead pass.

"Sure, I'm curious. How could I not be? You're my sister," Shannon says, and gives me a little shove in the back. I throw myself forward, like she's just pushed me hard, but the refs don't buy it.

I square up to face Shannon and laugh. Then I pivot while holding the ball with my elbows wide to create some space. "Sister? You officially need help." I try to drive right, toward the basket, but she stays in front of me and cuts off my driving lane.

"Have you ever wondered where your dad goes every Sunday?" she says, hands way up.

Not that it's any of her business, but Daddy drives out to Waller to visit his parents' graves every Sunday. I look to shoot, but I can't get a shot off with her crowding my space. I've already picked up the ball, so I can't put it down again without double dribbling. I look to pass, but no one is open.

The ref blows the whistle and points three fingers toward Langham's goal. *Shit, three-seconds.*

"Come on, Carli!" Jordan yells at me with her face scrunched up.

"My bad, my bad," I reply, and look at the scoreboard. Eighty-seven to seventy-seven with five minutes left on the clock.

"It's not your fault you don't know," Shannon says, running back toward her goal. "I only found out a couple years ago when I saw you play in the All-American game on TV. Saw Daddy cheering for you in the stands—"

"Daddy?" I interrupt, and give her a hard shove. This girl has really lost her mind. She thinks she's me. Like, I may need security after the game.

She shoves me back. "Yeah, at first I wondered why he was there. But it wasn't hard putting two and two together with me and you looking so much alike. He denied it at first. But when I pressed, he admitted it . . . made me promise to never tell or he would stop coming to see me," she says, straight faced, standing out beyond the three-point line.

I know she's only trying to distract me, but I wish she'd shut up. I've never seen her make a three, so I play off her a little and try to ignore all the nonsense she's talking. She's probably trying to clear the way for their point guard to run a pick and roll with their post. And after my last mess up, I want to be ready to help.

Their point guard passes to Shannon, and Shannon readies herself to shoot. I throw up my hand and yell,

"Copycat!" Super trite at this point, but it's the only thing I have time to think of. Doesn't work. Her three drops.

Coach Hill calls a time-out.

"Shame you have to make up such elaborate lies to get a shot off," I say before walking toward the bench.

"Ask your mom," she replies. "She knows. My mom finally called her and told her about a month ago."

About a month ago, I think. That's when all this drama started going down with the divorce. Well, five weeks, but still.

"Hustle up, Carli!" Coach yells. When I get close, she hands me a bottle of water. I squeeze it all over my face, hoping to wash Shannon's words away. Coach leans in close to me, so close I can smell the spearmint gum in her mouth. "We're almost there, Carli. But you have to give it your all these last few minutes. Do you hear me?"

I nod my head yes.

"Are you tired? Do you need to rest?"

I shake my head no.

"Well, I need you to get your head in the game. They're closing our lead," she says, and turns to speak to the whole team huddled around her.

I look up at Daddy, sitting in the third row, halfway between our bench and Langham's bench, but he's not looking at me. I follow his eyes over to Shannon. She's standing over her team drawing on the clipboard like she's the coach or something. I swear I hate that girl.

But Daddy looks like . . . like he's proud of her. I know that face—soft and bright, mouth stretched wide over a concealed smile. *Wait, she's not wearing my number. She's wearing his old number.* I look down at the twenty-two on my own jersey and remember him telling me as a kid that he'd be honored if I continued the Alexander legacy.

"Carli!" Coach Hill shouts. "Have you heard anything I said. What the hell is wrong with you? The championship game is on the line and you're over here daydreaming? Vanessa, go check in. Carli, take a seat."

I don't even protest.

I sit here and watch as Shannon takes it to Vanessa. Back dooring her, posting her up, and taking every rebound. I sit here and watch as we go from being up seven to five to two to none.

With less than a minute left on the clock, Coach Hill looks down the bench at me, ready to put me back in the game, ready for me to save the day. But I slump down in my chair and look away.

REX

Right, left, and jump. A simple-ass layup. But here I am spelling it out to myself, trying to keep my mind on the court and off Carli.

Head fake, crossover, pull up, and shoot. I miss. Halfway into my pregame warm-up, and I haven't seen her yet. After her team won (thanks to a last-minute three by Jordan) and everybody's family and friends rushed the court to celebrate the new champions, she wasn't there.

I was there. Even though I was still mad about her lying, I was in the middle of the court, wading the crowd, looking for her face. Waiting to pick her up and twirl her around—ready to celebrate. Cole, her mom, and her dad were looking for her, too.

You know what, forget seeing Carli. Good that she's off pouting somewhere just because she didn't get to play the last few minutes of the game.

Girls in royal blue warm-ups walk down the sidelines toward the stands. My eyes can't help but scan the line for big red hair. No Carli, so I sit down toward center court to stretch and look again. I hate myself for needing to see her. Why can't I get her out of my head!

"You ready to take this ass-whooping?" a voice beside me asks. I already know who it is before I look: Russell Price. I didn't even see him stretching before I sat down.

I don't have time for this dude right now. Carli's team is taking their seats low in the stands. I scan them again for her face, but don't see her.

Did she leave? I think. No way. They save the joint trophy ceremony until the very end, so I know she's still in the building. Plus, her mom and dad are still up in the stands. Cole just left their dad and is walking toward their mom. He catches me looking at him, pumps his fist in the air, and yells something I can't hear. Something encouraging, I'd bet from his big grin.

I smile and give him a thumbs-up.

My father and Angie, sitting right below where Cole is walking, must think the thumbs-up is for them because they start to wave.

I wave back right before the game clock sounds.

"Shame you're about to disappoint your fans," Russell says, standing.

"At least I have fans," I say, get up, and scan the crowd one more time. Wait! There she is! Up in the middle of the stands. But why is she sitting with Langham? Damn, not her. Just that girl she was guarding who looks like her.

CARLI

Same height. Same nose. Same pale skin with freckles. Same red hair.

Every Sunday for as long as I can remember.

Daddy.

She called him Daddy.

Suddenly and swiftly crumbling the vision of my own.

I can't go out there. I can't look at that man who's lied to me my whole life. That man who hid a whole sister from me.

This shower stall isn't hiding anything. I'm sitting balled up in a corner with my tears, snot, and iPhone between an empty bottle of Dove bodywash and a rusty Venus razor. A nest of brown hair covers the drain. The moldy bottom edge of the beige shower curtain almost hides a used tampon, but it's not long enough. All signs of my shitty life.

So many years of hiding her in plain sight. I wipe my nose with the sleeve of my warm-ups.

According to Facebook, Shannon Alexander Jackson was born November eighth—about a year and a half after me and two months after Cole. A throwback Thursday post shows a baby photo of her at the hospital in her mom's arms. In the background there's a man ducking underneath the doorway, leaving the room.

How am I ever going to leave this stall? As nasty as it is, I wish it would swallow me whole, keep my life on pause.

What am I even going to say when I have to see him?

Should I ask him about all the times I asked to go with him on Sunday? All the times he said he needed to be alone.

Should I ask him why he had to cheat on Mom? While she was pregnant, at that.

Why he had to hide his other child? Man up, for God's sake!

How could he live with himself?

How could he sit in the stands and watch us slam into each other? Watch us use all the things he's taught us against each other.

Should I ask him who he was cheering for?

Does he call Shannon Angel-face, too?

Forget it, he can call her Angel-face all he wants. And she can call him Daddy. I don't want him anymore.

MAKE
IT
STOP

● REX ●

I can't even be bothered with giving the play-by-play. We lose. Terribly. Russell Price scores thirty-seven. I score twelve. Couldn't get anything to drop. Couldn't get Carli out of my head. And now I want to erase her. Straight up. I want to find and destroy every little bit of her inside of me. Make it like I never caught her. Never kissed her. Never felt her. Never loved her. Like we were never anything.

CARLI

"Carli!" A locker bangs shut. "You need to bring your ass, Carli! I know you're in here. I see all your stuff." It's Jordan. Sounds like she's in the changing area. "Yo, we need to go! Everybody's waiting on us." And she's getting closer.

I squeeze my eyes shut like it's going to magically make me disappear. Stupid, I know, but I can't go out there.

More banging as she kicks the bathroom doors open one by one. The screech of metal rings sliding on metal bars as she flings back the shower curtains.

Now she's standing over me. "Get up!" she says, hands on her hips like she's somebody's mama. "You're not about to miss the award ceremony just because you didn't play the last few minutes of the game."

Is that why she thinks I'm in here? But I can't correct her. What am I going to say? *Oh, Shannon is actually my sister. My dad fucked her mom and hid her from us all these years.*

"What kind of sick shit is this?" she says, stepping over the used tampon. She grabs my arm. "I'm not playing, Carli. You need to get up."

But there's no way she can make me move. I'm way bigger than her.

"Okay, fine, then," she says, picks up the razor, throws it into the shower stall across the aisle, and sits down. "If you're missing it, I'm missing it."

"Jordan, no. Go," I say.

"I'm not going anywhere until you get up."

"You're being stupid. Go." Basketball means everything to her. No way she's going to miss the championship award ceremony because of me. And I know she's going to get the MVP.

"Me? I'm being stupid? I'm not the reason we're in here."

"Just go, Jordan. Please. Leave me alone," I say, feeling an onslaught of tears rush down my face. There's no way to stop them. All I want to do is stay in here. I'm not ready to face the truth, the lies, that man I used to call Daddy.

"It's not that serious, Carli," Jordan says, and puts her arm around me. She's never this affectionate. But I guess I've never been sitting in a nasty shower stall crying, either. "We won," she continues. "So what if that weird *Single Black Female* girl got the best of you for a few plays. Nobody's game is perfect."

I don't know what I'm supposed to think about Jordan talking about Shannon like that. Am I supposed to defend her like a good big sister? Am I supposed to join in trashing her because I can't stand her, because she just tore my world apart? Trying to decide how to feel is making my head hurt, my heart hurt, my everything hurt. I squeeze my eyes shut.

"Come on, Carli," she says, and puts her head on my shoulder. "I really don't want to miss this."

"I really don't want you to miss it, either," I say, sounding like some kind of whimpering dog.

She stands up, pulling me along with her, and I let her, thinking of the ways my body can be out there while my mind stays in here. On pause.

REX

About damn time. Carli is walking across the gym with Jordan. The captains of the other three teams have been standing in the center of the court for over ten minutes waiting on them. Russell Price and his point guard up on a winning platform posing for pics and shit, and me down here with the losers.

It's bad enough Carli made everybody wait on her, but this girl has the nerve to still be pouting. Her head is down so far I can't even see her face. Only hair.

She's coming up beside me, walking so close behind Jordan, I keep thinking she's going to step on a heel and pull off one of her sneakers. I swear to God, she better not say anything to me because I'm not hearing it. *Nah, baby girl. Not this time. No more letting you do me wrong while I'm over here giving 110 percent. You got me messed up.*

Now she's in front of me. So close that strands of her hair practically tickle my nose. A part of me wants to lean into it, put my face in it. Nah, fuck her good-smelling hair. I hold my breath, stop taking her in, and she passes me without even looking in my direction.

"Let's all give a big round of applause for all the championship teams," Jim Morrison, chairman of the Texas High School Basketball Association since forever, says as Carli and Jordan walk up the platform stairs. White dude has to be pushing ninety.

Most of the arena has emptied out. But the people left, mostly friends and family of the teams, give us their best—clapping, yelling, and stomping on the bleachers. My father and Angie are both clapping with their hands above their heads.

It almost makes me smile before I remember how terrible I played. How bad we lost. How much I embarrassed myself in front of everybody, including the college scouts. The look on Coach Bell's face. I've never seen a coach so disappointed in me.

Jim recognizes the sponsors and moves on to the trophies. He starts with the small ones, for the losers. "Langham High," he says, and picks up a small gold basketball with a wooden base off the folding table behind him.

The Langham team stands up off the visiting bench to the left. And the red-headed Langham girl, to my right, walks up on the platform to accept to the trophy.

"You all played a great game," Jim says to the whole team. Then he hands the trophy to the girl and says, "I'm looking forward to seeing big things from you in the years to come, young lady."

Meanwhile, Carli's head is *all* the way down. She could at least look up and be a good sport. Shake the girl's hand like Jordan and say something generic like *Good game*. Doesn't matter if she means it or not. That's what good athletes are supposed to do. But she's standing there playing with the zipper on her warm-ups. So damn self-centered.

"And Woodside High," Jim says.

I guess it's my turn. I wait for the Langham girl to come down.

"Being runner-up at this level is no small feat. It takes a fierce dedication to your sport and a strong commitment to excellence," Jim continues as I walk up the steps.

As I'm accepting the small-ass, loser-ass trophy, Carli, who's standing to the left of Jim, looks up at me. I look back at her, wanting something from her I wish I didn't want. I don't even know what. Maybe a look that says, *I'm sorry you lost* . . . or *I'm sorry I wasn't there for you* . . . or *Are you okay?*

But it's like she's looking right through me. Like I'm not even here. Like I don't even matter. Man, I'm so fucking stupid. I don't know when I'm going to get it through my thick head that this girl could care less about me. I look away and try to brush it off. But the hurt isn't going anywhere.

Russell Price, standing to Jim's right, reaches out to shake my hand and says, "It was close."

I swear to God I want to pop this dude in the mouth, but I shake his hand and say, "It won't be, next year."

"Yeah, we'll see about that," Russell says, and takes a step toward me.

Is this dude serious? He wins and all of a sudden he thinks he can step to me? "We sure will," I say, and stand an inch away from his face.

"And here we have the winning champion and MVP

of the Texas Boys State Championship," Jim says, overly cheery. He grabs Russell's arm and raises it toward the bright lights overhead. Yeah, Jim knows what's up. Knows he needs to save Russell from getting beat down.

But I still have to walk off the stage with the little-ass trophy.

CARLI

The winning trophy, a big gold basketball going through a gold hoop, is lighter than the one from freshman year. Looks the same, but they must've ordered it from a different company. Somewhere cheaper. And there's a huge scratch running along the top of it.

"Let me see it," Jordan says.

I reluctantly hand it to her. That's what I get for criticizing it, but I needed something to occupy my eyes. I can't look up. I can't risk seeing Shannon or her daddy and losing it up here in front of everyone.

Jordan lifts the trophy above her head, the crowd erupts in cheers, and our whole team rushes the stage.

"Yeah, that's right. Get up here and get your hands on this trophy!" Jim shouts over all the commotion. "You've earned it."

I take a step back. And back and back and back, letting my team pile in front of me, grateful for the opportunity to fade away.

"Carli Alexander," Jim says loudly into the microphone. I can't even see him with everybody on stage. "Get back up here, Carli."

Why? I think and hide myself behind Vanessa.

"Now, here we have a young girl," Jim says, and all of a sudden, his cold, bony arm is around my arm, leading me back to the front. "A young girl who's led her team to not one but two championships. A girl who's averaged a double-double her whole high school career, and in this game alone scored thirty-three points."

Did I? I think, looking high up in the arena where no one's sitting. Better than staring at the zipper, especially with all eyes on me.

"And she's only a junior. So I'm sure we'll see her back here next year, trying to lead her team to victory again. And that's why I'm so proud to award Carli Alexander with the MVP of the Texas Girls' Basketball Championship."

What? Jordan was supposed to get MVP. She hit the

winning shot. She's the reason we even made it to the championship. She led the team when I was out with my gallbladder surgery. I didn't even play the last few minutes of the game.

Jim places a gold statue of a girl shooting in my hands. *This isn't mine,* I think before I turn and start looking around for Jordan. But I can't find her and accidentally glimpse Shannon instead. *I can't. I just can't,* and I turn my eyes back up toward the empty stands.

REX

Look at you. Center stage. Holding your big, golden trophy. Just like you've never dreamed. Oh, but you like it, I see! Your nose way up in the air. I swear I hate you. You don't give a shit about my dreams. You don't care that I took a beating in the championship game because I was worried about you. You don't care that I probably lost my chance to go to a top school because of you. You haven't even looked in my direction. I mean, it's bad enough that you weren't there for me. But no words for me, either? Not even the silent, private kind? I swear you're worse than my father ever was. Maybe he never loved me all these years, but at least he had the decency to not pretend. Why pretend? Why tell me you loved me? So I could give myself away? So you could take and take and take? Well, I'm gone.

CARLI

"Your ass doesn't even like basketball!" Rex yells. I hear him before anyone else does. He's standing down below, to the left of the stage, staring at me with a hate so fierce it shoots straight through me.

I want to scream, *What are you doing? Shut up!* but shock has severed the connection between my brain and mouth.

Palming the small, gold basketball with his right hand, Rex sharply points the base of his trophy up at me. "You're such a fucking fraud!"

His words suck every sound out of the gym, and now all eyes are on him.

"Standing up there with that trophy when you know you hate basketball!"

Collective whispers and gasps from the crowd.

"Okay, I think that's enough," Jim says into the microphone, standing to my right.

But that doesn't stop Rex. "How you gon' be somebody's MVP when you're about to quit the team?"

Stop! Please stop! I plead with my eyes.

"Your ass ain't even playing next year. You don't deserve—" Rex's coach yanks him by the elbow and starts to march him toward the locker rooms.

A loud buzz from the crowd. Phones out recording.

My forehead feels clammy and I want to throw up.

"Well, folks . . ." Jim pauses, like he's trying to find the right words. "Emotions can run high at times like these. Why don't we give all the athletes another round of applause."

A few claps, but the buzzing drowns them out.

"I think we've all had a heck of a night," Jim says over the noise. "Let's be safe getting home."

I look back over my shoulder and see Rex and his coach disappearing into the tunnel leading to the locker rooms, the sting of his betrayal still piercing every inch of my skin. Those were my secrets to tell. Not his. Why would he do this? And in front of everyone?

I close my eyes, head reeling with confusion, and

imagine the last time I saw him, cheering wildly for me in the stands. *What the hell happ*— Damn, I missed his game. With everything going on, I wasn't even thinking about him. And he lost. In front of all the scouts.

Jordan grabs my shoulder and I turn around. "Is it true?" she asks, face screwed up with confusion.

"I was going to tell you——"

"Wait, are you serious? You're really quitting the team?"

"Yes, but——"

"I can't believe this shit! How could you keep this from me?"

"I wanted to tell you. I just——"

"Yeah, whatever," Jordan says, and walks off the stage. The rest of the team follows.

I forget to be careful and catch Shannon's daddy looking at me from the stands like I'm the biggest disappointment ever.

Even coming from him, I can't help feeling like I am.

● REX ●

Nothing hurt. In the gym, in my haze of anger, I felt numb. Free. But heading back to Houston in the backseat of my father's Tesla, it feels like I just had a bad dream.

If only I had.

If only my mind—suspicious of itself, unwilling to believe I did what I did—was right.

Why did I have to do Carli so wrong?

Well, she did me wrong first. I didn't hurt her more any more than she hurt me.

I can't believe I'm sittin' up here defending myself. Another warm tear slides down my cheek, and I quickly wipe it with my funky warm-up sleeve.

Angie slides hand over hand over hand, like she's washing them. And I wish I could wash myself of myself—scrub my conscience clean.

Then she turns back to look at me over her left shoulder, her black wavy hair framing her face, and says, "People make mistakes, Rex. You were upset. You can't beat yourself up about it."

But that's exactly what you should do. My ass could use a good beatdown right about now.

My father looks at me in the rearview mirror. "Yeah," he says, "give it some time. Things will blow over."

Blow over? This shame I feel isn't blowing anywhere. It's clinging to every thought and feeling inside of me. I can't feel hurt without the shame. I can't feel sorry without the shame. I can't feel weak or stupid or sad or mad or disgusted or embarrassed without the shame.

I almost wish I hadn't run out of the locker room before the team came in and was riding back on the bus with them. Maybe they could curse and stare the shame out of me. Maybe Coach could continue yelling and finger-wagging the shame out of me. With the big bus engine rumbling beneath me and all the rage and disappointment piercing me, maybe the shame would seep out, little by little.

But there's no one sticking it to me in my father's car. No engine rumbling, either. The ride is smooth and silent. I try to hold on to the sound of the tires' revolutions, but it's too faint and I keep losing it to the shame.

I grab my headphones out of my backpack, blast J. Cole, and lean my head against the window, wishing I could run out into the darkness. Wishing I could run and run and run and never come back.

CARLI

No way I was riding home with the team. No way I was riding home with that man, either, even though it's his weekend to have Cole and me. After the award ceremony, I didn't even go near him. I rushed up to Mom, told her I knew about Shannon, and begged her to get me out of there.

Riding home in her Discovery, I have to ask, "All those years and you never knew?" I've never imagined Mom as the kind of woman who could pretend to be blind, but maybe I don't know her like I think I do. Wouldn't be the first time I got a parent all wrong.

"No," she says, briefly taking her eyes off the dark road to look at me.

I let out a breath I didn't even realize I was holding. "You never even suspected?"

"No. I mean, I always knew your dad was dealing with things he didn't want to share with me. But I always thought it was related to the pain around his parents' death, you know. And I thought I could help him, love him through it, you know."

I do know, because I thought I could do the same for Rex.

"I tried for years to get close to his pain, to try to help him heal it, but he always stayed guarded and we'd end up fighting. I even suggested he see a therapist, but he refused. So I left it alone, you know, left him to deal with it himself. But I had it all wrong. I never . . . ever ever ever would've guessed that he had a"—her voice breaks up—"a child he was seeing every week for the last fifteen years . . . a child born during *our* marriage."

Mom's pain envelops me like a thick fog. I can't imagine being married to a man for twenty years and finding out he had a secret child for most of them. I can't imagine getting that call from the other woman. And who is this other woman? How long was the affair? A night? Five years? I have questions, but there's no way I'm hitting Mom with them right now.

Mom takes one of her hands off the steering wheel to wipe her eyes.

"I can drive," I offer.

"No, I'm okay," she insists.

I grab her free hand and hold it.

"He still loves you, you know," she says.

As always, here she goes trying to turn the spotlight off her pain, around to mine. "But what about you? Do you think he still loves you?"

She puts both hands back on the steering wheel. "Love is not just some feeling, Carli."

Her voice isn't normal. It's not hard like she's pissed or high like she's annoyed, but it's not normal.

"There's a deep responsibility to it . . . a deep trust. And no matter how your dad *feels*, he's failed to love me."

It's defiant. That's what her voice is. She wipes her eyes again.

"And he can be mad about me divorcing him so quickly all he wants, but there's no way I will ever be able to trust him again. And I can't be married to someone I can't trust. Don't need time or marriage counseling to tell me that."

An image of my parents sitting in a room on opposite ends of a light-blue sofa pops into my head. And another one of them sitting closer on the sofa. And then together in the middle of the sofa with Cole and me on either end. "You don't even want to try?" I ask.

"Try?" she says, her voice going high.

"Yeah, try couples counseling," I say, pushing past her annoyance. You see, the scared part of me doesn't care about her annoyance. Or about betrayal or the responsibility and trust of love. The scared part of me doesn't care about how much that man has hurt Mom. Or me for that matter. All it cares about is me staying intact. Less ground shifting beneath my feet. Keeping my family together, my life together—myself together.

"Look, you may not understand it, Carli. But I've made my decision. Everybody has to live their life making choices for themselves, choices that will hopefully lead to happiness. We may get it wrong sometimes, but all we can do is our best. And this is me doing my best. I need to move forward, and this is the only way I know how."

"Well, I'm gonna move forward and divorce him, too."

"You say that like it's easy."

"Well, it looks easy enough for you."

"What do you want me to do, Carli? Cry forever? Stay in pain forever? That's no way to live. I love myself too much for that."

Love myself. I wish I knew what that felt like. I don't even know myself. How can I love what I don't even know?

"And there *is* no divorcing your dad."

"You sound like you've never heard of people divorcing their parents."

"Look, Carli. Clearly your dad has some work to do on himself—"

"You can say that again."

"But that doesn't change the fact that he's your dad. He loves you. You don't want to throw away that relationship."

"But she calls him Daddy."

"Shannon?"

"Yeah."

"Well, he's her dad, too."

"Well, she can have him. I don't want him anymore."

"Look, Carli," Mom says, and briefly reaches over to touch my thigh. "Your dad will always be your dad. Yes, he has another daughter. But that's a fact you're going to have to accept. You have every right to be shocked and angry and hurt. But at the end of the day, none of that will change what *is*. You need to talk to him. Tell him how you feel. Make him tell you what you want to know about the situation."

"But he's a liar," I say, feeling my heart swell up in my throat and warm tears run down my cheeks. I turn to look outside the window at the darkness on the side of the road, hoping for some kind of sign. But the darkness won't say anything.

"Yeah, but you can still talk to him. One of the reasons he probably lied all these years is because he was scared of losing our marriage. But that's already gone."

If only I could be gone.

IT
ALL
COMES
DOWN

REX

I have eight missed calls from *My Love* when I grab my phone off my nightstand the next morning. Ten a.m. and I'm still in bed. On weekends the sun usually wakes me up, but it's not out today. On the other side of my glass sliding door, dark clouds creep across the sky.

I tap *My Love* on my phone and change it back to *Carli*. Then I scroll down to the bottom of her contact page and press *Block This Caller*. I know I need to apologize, but I'm not ready to talk to her yet.

Outside, the pines are bending to the wind. I swing my legs over the edge of the bed and slide my boxer briefs on—ready to step outside and take in the smell of the coming storm, ready to feel its force against my bare skin—when

I notice an envelope in the middle of my floor.

My father must've slid it underneath my door this morning. Wait, that means my father must've come upstairs. I've never seen him upstairs. Maybe he even knocked on my door when I was asleep. Maybe it's a letter from him saying all the things that still need to be said.

I wipe the crust out of the corners of my eyes and go pick it up. It's light purple. Not exactly my father's style. Plus, it has a stamp in the upper right-hand corner. Typed underneath a strip of teal tissue paper in the upper left-hand corner, it reads *Carli Alexander*.

I think about tossing the envelope outside and letting the rain wash her words away, so I'll never be able to take them in. But I don't. Instead, I sit down with the envelope in the middle of my cold wooden floor and bring it to my nose—exactly the thing I shouldn't do. But it smells like her, and I can't help but to breathe it in deep.

Doesn't mean anything. After I apologize, I'm still done with Carli.

Each line of her return address, of my address, is typed underneath alternating strips of lime-green and teal tissue paper, which are all pasted on the envelope separately. She probably spent over an hour on the envelope alone. The least I can do is open it and see what's inside. It's not like it's going to change anything.

I poke my pinky finger in the corner of the backside of the envelope, slide it underneath the triangular flap, and lift it up. First thing I see is our faces in front of a big, swirly sun. I quickly close the flap and push the envelope away from me, back underneath the door. I've already seen too much.

CARLI

The thunder outside my window sounds like it's ripping open the sky (not a good sign) as I call Rex for, like, the hundredth time. *Come on, Rex. Pick up the phone!*

I need to tell him about Shannon. I need him to understand why I missed his game. And he needs to know how much he hurt me by telling my secrets. Both of us need to apologize. And forgive. And afterward I need to slip in some of Mom's words about trust and responsibility, so our love can move forward toward something better.

I sit up in bed, hoping that a more upright position will somehow make him answer, and press ♥ Rex ♥ again.

Pick up! But there's only one ring before the computerized voice mail. More tears burning at the back of my throat find their way out.

Another knock at my door and I wipe the warm tears off my cheeks.

"Carli, I've got hot chocolate on the stove and it's getting cold." Mom's muffled voice comes through with N.E.R.D. playing in the background. First the doughnuts were getting cold with Missy Elliott. Then it was the blueberry scones with Mary J. She's been trying to get me out of my room with sugar and old-school hits all day.

I take a deep breath and manage to push out, "No thanks," without sounding like the hot mess I am.

"Okay, but you need to get something in your stomach."

"I will," I say in the most I'm-not-in-here-crying tone I can muster, hoping she'll be satisfied enough to go away.

She is.

My phone pings and my heart leaps with hope. But it's only a text from Cole. **U okay?**

Yeah I answer, and it's not even a complete lie. Hearing from Cole is actually right on time. I miss him. I know we've only been separated for one night. But I need his overly loving presence around me right now.

Too bad he's stuck on the other side of town with that man. Shame he doesn't know the truth about him yet.

So u really done with ?

Yeah

Why didn't u say something?

Thought you'd be disappointed

Come on . . . u know u can tell me anything

Yeah . . . but I know how much you love basketball

I hope u know I ❤ u more

Oh my gosh. I wish he was here to give me one of his hugs. I swear I would let him hold me forever. **I know ❤❤❤**

U need me to kick Rex's ass for u?

No but you can get him to pick up the phone

U still wanna talk to him after what he did 2 u??

I missed his game

Still! But that was pretty messed up. Where were u?

Locker room

R u serious???

There's stuff you don't know

Like what?

I think about telling him about Shannon. But I can't be the one to crush him. His dad needs to do that. **Can't tell you now but promise we'll talk soon**

What is it?

Can't say right now. Anyway Rex isn't picking up. Called 100 times

A little much don't u think?

But I need to talk to him

U need to stop calling

But I really need to talk to him

Trust . . . stop calling him & he'll call u

Fine, I text, swing my feet around to the floor, and stand up, thinking about how good those blueberry scones are about to be.

U saw the video?

I sit back down. **What video?**

Nothing. Don't worry about it

Tell me

It's nothing

Come on, Cole, I text, feeling myself getting mad.

Somebody filmed Rex's meltdown last night

What?

Yeah . . . already has over 200k views. A snippet even made ESPN.

Seriously??? Was it really that newsworthy?

U know ppl love the drama

U made up your mind about where u wanna stay? Gotta talk 2 the judge in a few days

Staying with Mom

Dang . . . still staying with Dad

A light somewhere inside me goes out. **I thought we were going to stay together**

Come live with Dad

I can't

Well I can't live with Mom

Why?

Why can't u live with Dad?

If only he knew. I catch a picture of the man I formerly called *Daddy* on my wall beside this gold-foiled starfish I made. He's in Galveston sitting in a beach chair with sunglasses and a hat on. The back of my legs got stung by a jellyfish that day, and Mom had to rub meat tenderizer on me to soothe my stings. If only my wounds had such a simple remedy now. **Come on Cole** is all I can think to write back.

Come on Carli

Seriously??? So we're going to live in different houses and go to different schools? You know I'm only going to be here for one more year

Trust me . . . I know

I don't have a comeback for that. Only tears.

After a couple minutes, he texts again. **Sucks but everything will be okay**

Why do people always say that? It's, like, the biggest lie .

REX

When I go downstairs, the TV in the living room isn't on and there's a note on the kitchen counter from my father saying he got called in. On a Sunday, though? Couldn't he have said no? Blamed it on the storm? I mean, he saw what went down yesterday. He knows today has to be rough.

Clearly that doesn't matter to him, just like my game didn't matter to Carli. I don't know why I keep fooling myself into believing that anyone actually cares.

After eating three bowls of Honey Nut Cheerios while watching the rain come down on the trees in sheets, I head back upstairs. In the hall, outside my door, the purple envelope is waiting on me like it knew I would be back sooner or later. Like it knew I'm so pathetic that I would eventually need whatever love it has to give.

I pick it up and carry it into my closet, where I feel

safer. I lay it on my dresser, remembering Carli the night she sat here—her face, her lips, the new places I kissed and touched her.

I slip out the card. It's handmade and looks like a collage. On the front, Carli's handing me an orange-looking flower, and purple rays shoot from her chest to mine. I can't even lie—it's beautiful and it feels like magic. Like love is really flowing from her heart to mine.

I know I should put the card down, but I can't. I open it.

A whole page of her words that look like art. Handwritten letters that bend and loop and stay straight in curious places. *Ls* that never want to be lowercase. *Ts* that never want to be the same—short, straight, long, curvy, and crooked strokes crossing at wide-ranging spots along stems, which sometimes curve up at the ends. I remember seeing her handwriting all over her walls, but looking at it now makes me feel like I'm seeing a part of her for the first time.

Rex,

I don't think it's possible to tell you everything in my heart. I don't have the words for it. Like if I tried, they wouldn't be enough

"I love you" isn't enough.

I swear loving you is the only thing saving me right now. You just don't know, this past month has been the worst time in my life (other than when I'm with you or talking to you or thinking about you). My whole world is falling apart. It's too much to write here, but I will say I haven't been handling it well. It's like I don't know what to do or who I am and it's making me feel crazy.

Sorry I took the bad stuff in my life out on you. You don't deserve it. I'll never treat you like that again. I promise. Please forgive me. I love you.

Yours forever (and the day after that, and the day after that),
Carli

I can't, I think, wiping tears from my face. *I just can't.* I leave the card in the closet and go get my phone.

CARLI

I finally see it. After single-handedly bringing the *Rex Carrington's Epic Tirade* video up to 300,000 views on YouTube, I finally understand. Rex never loved me. He couldn't have. He doesn't know love.

The anger on his face made one thing clear: all he knows is pain. Every square inch inside of him is drenched in it. He tries to hide from it, but there's no hiding. Tried to hide inside of me. He probably thought his hiding was love. I know I thought it was. And maybe I was hiding in him, too, I'll admit.

But no more. I'm out. Done with whatever this screwed-up thing is that he calls love. I can't do it anymore.

The booming thunder agrees. I'm still in bed, staring out my window, thoughts pouring down.

I deserve better than what he has to give.

Anyway, how could I ever trust him again after what he did to me?

I can't.

It's over.

My phone rings and I roll over in bed to grab it where I left it on my pillow, but it's not there. I quickly sit up and throw my Kantha quilt back, my sheet back. Still don't see it. Third ring. *This can't be happening.* I lift my pillow and my stomach growls in relief. Still haven't been out of my room to get those blueberry scones, but Cole was right. "Hello," I answer.

"Hi," Rex says, his voice as heavy as the rain coming down outside.

Hearing his tender voice puts me right back inside of him, and I send all the things I just told myself packing. I lie back down and reach to touch Rex's face on the wall right above my pillow. I have the picture of us on the sofa pinned up between a sketch of a sunflower forest and a line from Kahlil Gibran's *Prophet*.

All these things shall love do unto you that you may know the secrets of your heart,
and in that knowledge become a fragment of Life's heart.

I look at it every night before I go to sleep and every morning when I wake up, trying to figure out what it means.

"I'm sorry about the video. About what people are saying," I tell him.

"What video?"

"Never mind," I say, ready to play the tell-me game.

He doesn't press for more.

"And I'm really sorry for missing your game," I start to explain, "at the end of my game, Shannon—"

"Wait," he interrupts. "I just called to say I can't do this anymore. And I'm really sorry for what I did to you last night. It was wrong. I had no right. I was just so upset."

Clearly he can't mean what he's saying? I get it because I was just thinking the same thing, but I didn't mean it, either.

"You don't mean that," I say.

"Yes I do."

"No you don't."

"Yes I do."

"You're just upset. But if you let me explain—"

"Look, Carli. I mean what I said. I can't do this anymore. I was lonely before I met you, yeah. But I knew how to handle that. What I can't deal with is you loving me one minute and pretending you don't even know me the next. It's making me crazy," he says, and sniffs.

My heart disappears out of my chest as I try to decipher his words. "What do you mean loving you one minute? I've never stopped loving you. You don't understand—"

"Maybe you're right. Maybe I don't understand you. I thought I did, but really I don't have a clue what's going on inside you. But I can't keep trying to figure it out. It's messing up my life. I'm sorry, Carli, but it's over."

My heart is back, but it's a thousand-pound weight in my chest. I don't think my body can hold it. "What? No!" is all I can manage to say, tears strangling my words.

"I'm sorry, but I can't see you or talk to you anymore," he says, his voice cracking.

"Rex, please don't do this. I'm so sorry. I love you so much. I—"

"Nah, love isn't supposed to feel like this," he says, his voice firming up.

"I know. I'm sorry. Please let me explain—"

"Nah, man. Nah."

"But I thought you said you loved me."

"What? I poured it *all* out to you. Every little ounce of the love I had. You think you're the only one with problems?" His voice is hard. "Well, you're not. I'm dealing with some pretty fucked-up shit over here, too, Carli. Even still, I've always been there for you. From the very beginning. But you haven't done the same for me. And I've already heard all the apologies and *never again*s I'm going to hear. Look"—and he softens his tone—"I'm sorry. I just can't do this."

"Rex, give me a chance to explain," I beg.

"I'm sorry, Carli. I gotta go."

Dial tone.

I call him back.

One ring, voice mail.

Again.

One ring, voice mail.

Again.

One ring, voice mail.

Again and again and again with the rain pouring down outside my window.

Again and again and again until I'm coughing on my tears.

Again and again and again until I feel too stupid to keep calling.

He didn't even give me a chance to explain. I missed his game, yeah. But is that all it takes for him to throw me away? He's such a liar! He never loved me. He couldn't possibly have. If he loved me, he would've at least listened to me. He would at least pick up the phone. He wouldn't make me suffer like this. I swear I hate him.

I yank down the picture of us above my pillow. The forest of sunflowers. The Kahlil Gibran poem. Underneath it, there's a picture of our family in Kusama's *At the End of the Universe* exhibit. We're standing with our arms wrapped around one another in a small dark room at the center of tiny yellow lights that seem to stretch out infinitely. But ain't no more family! My walls are such a fucking lie!

I yank it down.

And the sketch of a silver flute I drew beside it.

And the handwritten Rihanna lyrics beside that.

I don't know who you think I am
I don't know who you think I am
I don't know who you think I am
I don't know who you think I am

And the trail of black stars drawn with various black marker tips underneath that.

And the picture of the Egyptian winged goddess, Isis.

All of the photos and quotes and ticket stubs and random written words and poems and facts and maps and magazine images and sketches and swatches of fabric and paper birds and birthday cards.

Every memory.

Oh, now the Mesopotamia fact wants to pop up. Written with purple crayon in perfect cursive. I hold it with two hands until sweat, pretending to be a tear, splashes on the curl of the capital *M* and reminds me of how all of this pain began. *Fuck the first kisses fact!* Off it goes to the floor with everything else.

Every love.

Every hope.

Every possible sign.

Until there's nothing left but scraps still holding on to tacks.

"Why are you still holding on? There's nothing left!" I scream, out of breath, and furiously start going after the last bits, ripping the tacks off the wall.

"Oh, Carli," Mom says behind me.

I didn't even realize she'd come in. She's looking around in disbelief. I've been putting things up on my walls since I was four, since first watching her tack up things on her design boards. And I haven't taken anything down since, just added layer over layer.

Until now.

And it's like I'm seeing my walls blank for the first time. Like they're closing in on me on all four sides, wanting answers about what I've just done. Whenever I used to look at my walls, it was like bits of my possible future staring back at me . . . but now there's nothing. What am I supposed to do with nothing? What is nothing supposed to tell me about everything?

● REX ●

Sitting in the middle of my hard, wooden floor, with the rain still pouring outside my windows, I search my name in YouTube. First new thing that pops up is a clip of the ESPN commentator Stephen A. Smith saying, "Since y'all wanna talk about Rex Carrington, when are you going to acknowledge that he just doesn't deserve the title you've given him. No. 1 high-school basketball player of the year? Puh-lease! And he's talking about what Carli Alexander doesn't deserve, who's a hell of a player, by the way. But can we get back to what he doesn't deserve?"

I swear I hate that dude. That smug look on his stupid, pointy face. He stays talking shit about somebody. Made a career out of it. Can somebody please tell me why people love to watch other people getting ripped to shreds?

I click on the clip below it: somebody's homemade video of me going off on Carli. It already has over 300,000 views. You can hear whoever's videoing in the background saying, "Oh shit! It's going down."

The video only plays for a few seconds before I press pause.

That's not me, I think. That dude whose eyes have no

tenderness. Whose mouth has no mercy. *Where did I go?*

I can't bring myself to watch anymore. Instead, I look through the comments.

mrmball

Rex is a fool. Definitely not top recruit material

Amara Queen

He just mad cuz he played terribly. Boy is so overrated

Lil Flacco

Has anyone else watched this 10+ times. Bruh, I swear I can't stop. Lol

Kasey C

That poor girl

Tarantula Girl

Her name is Carli Alexander. Put some RESPEK on her name

Wassup B

Dude is clearly off his pills

365BasketballTV

Check out my channel. BasicsofBallin

Trapgirl

Now this is good entertainment! Better than the Housewives of Atlanta

lifeonthecourt

Rex Carrington is still the truth. He does look like he needs therapy though

LisaLee529

It's obvious he's been hurt. You all need to leave him alone!

Blissfully Joi

Somebody needs to put a foot in his ass. Carli Alexander did not deserve that. If you don't know who she is, then look her up

Daquan

That was cold

That's not me! I throw my phone across the room, and it crashes into the glass box of beetles on my bookshelf. *Don't they get it? I'm not capable of that much cruelty!* It came out of nowhere, unfolding its brutal body inside of me. I couldn't stop it! And now *I'm* the one stuck with the mess. With people judging me, like they know me.

Nobody knows who I am!

Oh, but they've got their drama. They've got their views. And now coaches and scouts will have their reasons. And nobody will want me on their team! Is that what everybody wants? To see me lose everything? Well, they're in luck 'cuz it's gone. I can hang up going to the league after my first year of college. That dream is dead along with everything else.

Exhausted, I sit for long time, looking at the broken glass on my floor and the scattered beetles in between. When I was little, I used to stand on the ottoman to get them down from the top shelf in the living room. Then I'd hold them close to my chest while taking baby steps to the sofa, where I'd look at them for hours. I'd imagine Mom looking at them with me, telling me which ones were her favorites.

I look at a crack in the iridescent one's blue shell (her favorite). At the bright green beetle (her second favorite) and its thin, broken wing. At the purple-and-orange striped one who's now missing its antenna. At the black beetle on its back with only half of its jointed legs in the air.

Damn, after all these years, I can't believe I just messed up Mom's beetles, all because I got mad. Me. Not some kind of body snatcher who appeared out of thin air. Not the homie from way back when. I did this.

NEVER
WOULD'VE
IMAGINED

REX

After school I get back in bed. I'm rereading one of Mom's books about this dope landscape architect named Water Hood and listening to her Otis Redding album (trying to keep Carli, basketball, and the beetles out of my head), when I hear a knock at my door.

"Rex?" My father's soft voice slips under the door into my room. Just like it slipped in Sunday after he got home from the hospital, yesterday after school, last night before I went to bed, and this morning before school.

But my father isn't the only one who can ignore somebody. Who can stay in his room and pretend the person they live with isn't actually there. Who could care less.

"Rex?"

I don't answer.

"Rex?" My door opens slightly. Widens. My father takes a step into my room in his green scrubs. And another one. And another one until he's standing in the middle of my room looking around at all of Mom's things.

As if on cue, the record finishes and the needle lifts.

He looks over at me.

I look back at my book like he's not even there.

"What are you reading?" he asks.

I hold up my book so he can see for himself.

"Oh yeah. Walter Hood is something special, isn't he? The *Street Trees* he's doing in Detroit and the *W.E.B. DuBois Double Garden* installation he did with Carrie Mae Weems are amazing," he says, and walks over toward my bookshelf.

Why is this man trying to act like he knows about Walter Hood?

"Your mom and I saw his installation at the Project Row House here in Houston when she was pregnant with you." He grabs the next record off the top of the stack— "What's Going On" by Marvin Gaye. Slides it out of its sleeve. "Do you mind?" he asks, his long fingers already lifting the needle to switch out the records.

Is he serious? This man is in my room, acting like he's been in here a thousand times. Over there casually mentioning Mom like we've had a million conversations about her. He never once talked about Mom! Never shared any stories about her. About what she was like. What they did. Where they went. Or what happened back when. Never! "Yes, I mind!" I shout.

"I'm sorry . . . I'm sorry," he says, gently places the needle back down, and slides "What's Going On" back into its sleeve.

"Sorry for what exactly?" I yell, standing to my feet with my fists balled up.

He turns to face me. "Sorry for—"

"For what?" I walk toward him, anger spewing out of me. It feels like a pipe—rusted, corroded, and under the pressure of being clogged for sixteen years—finally broke deep inside me. "Coming up in here acting all familiar? Or sorry for ignoring me all these years? For never being here?"

He looks up at me. He's tall, but I still have him by a couple inches. "Yes, for everything I—"

"Sixteen years! Sixteen years of leaving me on my own," I interrupt, screaming three inches from his face. "You know, I lost Mom, too. Actually, I never even had her. And I didn't have a father, either." Specks of spit fly out of my mouth, but I don't give a damn. "No, even worse.

I had a father who didn't want me. Who hated me. Didn't you know how much I already hated myself! I killed my own fucking mom! I've had to live with that!" Hot tears are streaming down my face and I don't try to hold them back.

"Oh no. Is that what you think?" he says, and reaches out to me.

I block his arms and step back. "Man, get off me."

"Rex," he says. "You have to know, it's not your fault," his voice soft and calm.

It's how he always talks, but right now it's on my goddamn nerves. "You can lose the bedside manner. I'm not one of your patients."

"You were only a baby. It's not your fault."

"Yeah, yeah, yeah. You can save all that."

"Rex, listen to me. I think your mom had some kind of undiagnosed heart condition. I don't know for sure because there were no further investigations done at the time. But we know a lot more about the dangers of undiagnosed heart problems in pregnancy these days."

The words *undiagnosed heart condition* stretches out inside me beside my guilt. And my guilt eyes it, sizing it up like I do when a new dude rolls up on the basketball court with the same build as me or the same height as me or the same shoes as me (basically with anything like me).

"Did I do this? Do you think it's your fault because of me? I'm so sorry. I've been such an awful father," he continues. "Your mother would've been so disappointed in me." He looks down briefly and then right back up, eyes full of tears. "Look, I've done a terrible job loving you, but you need to know it's not your fault. You were only a baby. It's a miracle you've turned out as amazing as you have. I just didn't know how," he says, his voice cracking. His tears start to fall.

"Nah, you don't get to cry. You were the adult! I was the child!" I scream, feeling *It's not your fault* trying to find its way deeper inside of me.

"I know, I know. I'm sorry. I checked out. And after being checked out for so long, I didn't know how to get back to you. How to talk to you. I was so depressed. Every time I saw you, I saw her. Even right now, looking at you, I see her. Her cheekbones. Her moles. The way she always slightly held her head to the side. The same pure look in her big eyes."

My father's words stun me. *Me look like Mom? Nah.* When I was a little boy, I used to be obsessed with looking at Mom's pictures. At her face, her outfits, her hair, her poses, her surroundings—anything that would clue me in about who she was. But after I realized her pictures ran out the day she gave birth to me, I stopped looking at them. And shortly thereafter, I stopped looking at myself. And now standing here, I can't really picture either one of us.

I back away from my father, walk over to my file cabinet, open my bottom drawer, and take out the white wooden box that houses Mom's old photos.

On top of the stack, there's a picture of her posing in front of a brick wall painted like pixels. She's sporting an afro with her arms on her hips and her head tilted to the side. She's a lot lighter than I am. And shorter. I can't see it.

"You got everything from your mom," my father continues. "The only thing you got from me was height and a little color. None of my personality, thankfully. Your mom was super passionate, like you. About life, about art . . . all kinds of art. And she loved trees. I mean, she really loved trees."

I always knew Mom loved trees. Well, I didn't know-know. It was the version of her I made up from this one picture I used to love. I start sliding photo off of photo, trying to find it. Here it is: Mom sitting crisscross in the grass in a grove of live oaks. Looking at her, looking up at the trees, I get the same feeling as when I'm lying in the woods behind the house, looking up at the crowns of the tall pines. It's the closest I ever get to peace.

"That's why I moved us out here to live among all these trees," my father says, walking closer to the sliding glass door. He interlaces his fingers behind his back and stares out at the hazy forest. "I thought waking up surrounded by trees every day would make you happy."

The subject of moving takes me right back to being pissed. "I was happy around Mom's old things. In the house she used to live in," I yell, stepping toward him. "I used to imagine her walking through the rooms. I used to imagine her sitting on our old sofa and cooking in our old pots and pans. That made me happy. This house is empty and sad. You didn't keep anything of hers. It's like you wanted to get rid of her," I say.

He turns around to face me. "No, no, no. I would never want to get rid of your mom. I love her. Always. My therapist thought it was critical that I move out."

"Your therapist?"

"Yes, he's been imploring me to move for years and years, and then something happened that made me listen."

"But you didn't even ask me first," I say, wondering what happened.

"I know. I'm sorry. I was in a really bad place. And I needed to get out quickly. Every second in that house brought back memories. Trust me, I would've stayed with those memories forever. But," he says, looking at me, "I had to keep living. I had to keep living for you."

Keep living? For a second my insides go black. Everything disappears, and I imagine being all alone in this world. Was he thinking about killing himself? Is that what happened? Even though he hasn't been there for me, the thought of losing another parent is unbearable.

"But I'm here. And I'm much, much better. And I promise to do better from here on out," he says, and reaches for me.

Part of me wants to fling my arms open and run to him, yelling *Daddy* like I'm five years old. But the anger, still seeping out beneath my skin, won't let me.

He walks toward me and wraps his arms around me. And now he's holding me for the first time I can remember. It's weird, I know he's trying to give me love. Love that I need. Shit, love that I've been wanting my whole life. But I can't feel anything.

CARLI

Judge Reed's chambers are creeping me out with all the dead animals. Beside her desk there's some kind of wild cat with a bird stuffed in its mouth. On the floor, in front of a wall of legal books, there's a ram's skull and horns surrounded by large bones. By the window there are two wolves on posts, heads up, like they're howling at the moon. And on the opposite wall—above the giant map of Texas—there's a duck with its wings spread, trying to fly away from it all.

Maybe a sign that I should try to get the hell out of here, too. But how?

The judge is leaning on her large mahogany desk, short legs stretched to the floor, holding a pen and legal pad. On almost every finger, she has some kind of expensive-looking ring. She's wearing dark jeans, cowboy boots, a light pink blouse, and a string of pearls underneath her black robe.

She's staring at me, wanting to know why I want to stay with Mom. I'm sitting in the leather armchair across from her trying to think of what to say. I'm not about to tell this judge about Shannon. Nuh-uh. I already know what she would write on her legal pad: *Black man had a baby by his sidepiece.* I mean, she probably wouldn't use *sidepiece*, but you know what I mean. Even though I hate him, I'm not about to let this little white lady reduce him to that.

"I'm just closer to my mom. She gets me," I finally answer.

"Can you elaborate, sweetie?" she asks, in her country (and when I say country, I mean *country*) voice.

I tell her about basketball and explain Mom is the only one I can talk to.

Judge Reed bites the inside of her left rouged cheek. "Are there other reasons? Besides basketball? It's really important you tell me all the reasons you want to live with your mom. It'll help me make a decision based on what I think is in your best interest."

"But I'm already telling you what's in my best interest," I say with more attitude than I want to.

She walks over and sits down beside me in the other leather armchair. "And I'll definitely take that into consideration," she says, and moves the vase of wildflowers from the round table between us to the floor. Judge Reed puts her pen and legal pad down on the table. The lined yellow pages are still blank. Then she props her elbow up on the table, rests her chin in the palm of her hand, and fixes her blue eyes on me. As if to say, *If you wanna stay with your mom, you'd better give up the goods.*

And I do. About everything that happened Saturday. About Sunday for as long as I can remember. About his lies. His double life. Let me tell you, the fear of the judge ordering me to live with that man has me spilling all the beans.

Judge Reed lifts her head. "Yeah, that's hard. I found out about my other siblings around your age, too." She leans back in her chair and puts her cowboy boots up on her desk. "That's when my mama died."

"I'm sorry," I say, surprised the judge has family drama like mine.

"Don't be, sweetie. We weren't close. You see, she left when I was a little baby . . . like four or five months old. Supposedly one of those big-time oil execs came into the IHOP where she worked, and she ran off with him. Left me and my daddy behind in Plainview and never came back. Never heard from her again," she says, and runs her fingers through her hair.

"Then one day," she continues, "I get this letter in the mail saying she died and left me and my siblings a whole bunch of money. My mama had three kids from her marriage with that rich man, you see. I didn't even know they existed. But now we've all been getting together for Christmas Eve dinner for some forty-plus years."

I picture myself having dinner with Shannon. Nope. Not happening. "But weren't you mad? I mean, your mom abandoned you and then went and raised all those other kids."

"I guess I could've been, but there's no use being mad at a dead woman. No use being mad at my siblings, either. They didn't do anything. Besides, all that money I got from my mama put me through college and law school. In a way, I probably wouldn't be where I am today if it wasn't for her running off."

The judge telling me all of her business has me feeling comfortable. So comfortable I think about putting my Blazers up on the desk to join her boots, but I don't. "True, true. But how can you still call her Mama?"

"Well, that's what she is, isn't she? What about your mama? You don't have grievances against her?"

The question throws me off. In all the sharing, I'd almost forgotten what we were here for. "I guess she works a lot," I answer, trying not to say too much. I need the judge to decide it's best for me to live with her.

"And that's okay with you?"

No one's ever asked me how I feel about Mom working so much, and now my words are trying to rush up and out, like someone just handed them a permission slip. "Well, I used to feel like her work was more important than me.

Like she loved it more than me or something. When I was younger, I used to hate staying in aftercare at school. And on top of that, I always saw other moms volunteering in the classrooms or organizing bake sales and stuff. My mom was never there. I mean, don't get me wrong, I was always proud of my mom. But I was also jealous of how much time her work took away from me."

"I understand. My kids felt the same way. When—"

"But now that I'm older I know she loves me more, no question about it," I interrupt, trying to turn my answer around before the judge goes on another talking spree. "But I also understand her work gives her something I can't give to her. And that's okay. I want something like that for my life, too. Basketball definitely isn't it. I'm still looking for it."

She takes her boots down off the desk, stands up, picks up her legal pad, and puts the flowers back on the table. "And you'll find it. I know you will."

Wait, is the interview over? I thought we were just getting started. I need to say more good things about Mom.

"Well, it was very nice talking to you. I have another appointment waiting, but I assure you I have everything I need to make a decision."

I look at the wild cat with the bird in its mouth and a strange pressure squeezes my throat. This lady wasn't being sweet and open. She was getting what she wanted—chewing me up. And now she's spitting me out.

Judge Reed walks toward the door and opens it. "Your parents should receive my ruling by the end of the week."

I want to beg her to let me live with Mom, tell her my whole life depends on it. But I stand up, say, "Okay, thanks," and walk out.

In the hallway Mom is sitting on a wooden bench on one side of the hall, Daddy (I guess I can call him that since that's what he is) is sitting on a bench on the other side of the hall, and Cole is standing in between. He met with the judge right before me.

And now Daddy is walking toward me. "You hungry?" he asks.

I shake my head and go try to sit beside Mom, like I've been doing all morning, but she stands up and walks closer to him.

I head toward my next safe place.

"How'd it go?" Cole asks, and gives me a hug.

"Okay, I guess," I say. "I don't really know."

"Yeah, same. Glad it's over, though."

"Me, too."

"You hungry? Because I'm starving."

"Yeah," I say.

Daddy appears over Cole's right shoulder. "Your mom and I thought it would be a good idea if you came to eat dinner with me and Cole went to eat with her."

Who thought what? I think, and shoot Mom an alarmed look.

Standing right beside him, she looks at me calmly and says, "It's for the best. Your dad can drop you back off at my house when y'all finish up."

She can't be serious. Why would she make me go with him?

"You ready, Angel-face?" he asks with a weak smile.

A bright flash of panic runs through me, and I think about taking off down the empty hall, about trying to get away from it all like that duck on Judge Reed's wall. But let's be real, the duck can't escape, and neither can I. I may not be stuffed with rags and cotton, but I'm stuck with Daddy for now.

REX

After my father leaves, I grab my phone off my desk, push the camera app, and flip it around to selfie mode. There's a bad crack traveling diagonally across the screen from when

I threw it across the room, but I can mostly see myself.

Still holding the picture of Mom, I bring our faces side by side. I can't believe I never saw it. Our strong cheekbones, our many moles, our hooded eyes—alike. Satisfaction quickly fills me up. But I keep staring, eyes floating back and forth between us until I'm in straight-up awe.

You see, I used to think of my moles as tiny sins, little reminders of what I did. But looking at Mom's moles is making them feel like tiny marks of sainthood or something. I know nobody's about to erect a statue of me in a sanctuary or anything, but looking at her face is making mine feel holy and bright. Like it's been washed clean.

But when I look up at the gray sky outside my window and back down at the big crack across the screen, I remember Mom's beetles belly up among broken glass. Man, I don't *even* want to think about that. But that doesn't stop my mind from going back to how heated I was when I hurled my phone. Or flashing to my tight fists dreaming of going upside my father's head.

Underneath the jagged line on the screen, the same angry face I saw on that video stares back at me. *Is this really me?* I swear to God that's why I don't even like looking at myself. All the stuff I try to keep buried is always trying to come up and make me feel something.

Why does everything have to keep coming up? Like what every coach and scout must think of me. *I know! I know!* And Carli. *But I've already apologized to her.* And the dream I lost—*hurts so bad it's sickening!* The anger that won't quit until everything I love is either broken or gone.

It has to stop.

I put Mom's picture down on my desk and lock eyes with myself. Man, I don't want to do this. I swear looking at myself makes my head and heart hurt. For a second I almost look away. Ready to get up and continue on with life like I always do, like everything is cool. But I can't even front like that's working anymore.

So I take a deep breath, blow it out slow, and force myself to keep staring at myself.

Until I can see past the crack in the screen into the face I always saw as my father's. Into the hate I always thought he had for me. The hate I always had for myself. I swear it's like a million wrecking balls swinging around, destroying everything inside of me. Feeling it is the absolute worst, but I'm not about to keep ignoring it and let it ruin me.

Tears rush down my face, and I wipe them and keep staring.

Until I see a little kid I haven't seen in years. Alone, playing with all his dead mom's things. A kid crushed by his father's absence and silence. A kid who spent all his time out of the house, either balling or under the tree out back talking to his mom and begging for her forgiveness.

I swear, the weight of it is enough to break me. But I square it up and make myself feel it. Tears dripping from my chin, I scoop up the little kid, squeeze him tight, and tell him what he's always wanted to hear, *It's not your fault.*

Over and over again.

It's not your fault.

It's not your fault.

It's not your fault.

Until I can feel the words sink into the innermost part of me.

Then I turn toward the pile of the injuries I've kept buried in me over the years. Every hurt I never wanted to feel. Still here.

But the closer I look at them, the more I see that most of them have nothing to do with me and everything to do with the people they came from. And after a while, most of them rise up, give me a few head nods (I think they like being seen), and start getting the hell up out of me.

I keep staring and staring until I'm in awe again. Of this dude with the two puffy eyes, snot-streaked lips, and flat, crooked nose. This dude who's been through some shit—I'm talking about some major shit—but who's still here, even after finally having the guts to take a good look at himself.

I swear I never thought looking at myself could feel like love. But it does.

CARLI

Tires crunching over gravel, I open my eyes to see what restaurant was worth the hour drive. But we're in a graveyard. First of all, I'm hungry. And second of all, really? He's never brought me here all these years I've been asking. All these years he's been lying about coming. But he wants to bring me now?

He turns the engine off, his million keys (I wonder if one of them opens the door to Shannon's house) hanging from the ignition. "I want to show you something," he says.

And? I think, but don't say a word. Hadn't said a word to him since we left the courthouse. I resume the position I had the whole way here: eyes closed behind dark shades, head against the window, thinking about Rex.

"Please, Carli," he says.

I keep my eyes closed, wishing he would shut up and take me to get something to eat.

"Come on, Carli," he says, a crow squawking in the background.

I wish they would both shut up. "Wake me up when we get to the restaurant."

"I'll take you right after we leave here, promise. It won't be long," he says, his voice perking up. I guess because I actually said something. *Oooo, I wish I would've kept my mouth shut.*

"Shannon told me what happened at the game. And I wanted to—"

Hearing her name leave his mouth is too real for me, and I quickly open the car door to get away from him, away from her. But as soon as I'm outside, this weird feeling hits me, like I've been here before.

It's that tree. Boy, would Rex love that tree. The one in the middle of the cemetery that looks like it's been here since the beginning of time. The live oak whose trunk looks ten feet wide. Whose long, winding, moss-covered branches extend way farther out than up, some dipping close to the ground. I know that tree.

I walk closer to it.

"You remember, don't you," Daddy says behind me.

I keep walking, and a picture flashes to the front of my mind of me swinging from a low branch. I was about two or three and Daddy yelled at me to get down.

"You're the only person I've ever brought here," he says, still walking behind me.

Then I see it. A tombstone right under the low branch engraved with *Camille Alexander*. His mother's name. But she's alone. She's supposed to be buried beside her husband.

Daddy kneels down in front of the tombstone. Below her name, it reads, *You will always be the girl of my heart, Love Randy.*

But that makes no sense. His parents both died in the same car accident.

I take off my shades so I can see better. The sky is as gray as these tombstones anyway.

When I look back down, Daddy's whole back is trembling, his shoulders shaking. I've never seen him cry. Sad, yes, all the time. But never crying. And all of a sudden it feels like my heart is opening on all sides, like I'm coming apart. Everything inside me wants to see what's hurting him. What's been hurting him my whole life.

I kneel down with him and put a hand on his back, and he lets more of it out, heaving and weeping. "My father lives twenty minutes outside of Austin in a town called Georgetown," he says, and briefly turns to me, his face redder than his freckles.

"What? I thought—"

"He wasn't in the car that night. He was with me," he says, still breathing like he just finished running a race.

I'm so confused that I don't know what to say. But I want to hear more. I need to hear more. So I sit down on the ground and grab his arm, encouraging him to do the same. It takes him a second to get his long legs crossed, but he does. And now we're sitting cross-legged in the grass facing each other.

"Him and Mommy were never married. He didn't even live with us," he says, his voice calming down. "They weren't even together that long. He couldn't deal with the disapproval of his family and friends. Couldn't deal with people staring at him walking down the street with a black woman."

What? I knew his dad was white, but I had no idea that his mom being black was a problem. I'd always imagined them living together in their own happy bubble.

"He used to drive down from Georgetown to see me every Sunday. Mommy would usually cook and do things around the house while he played with me. The night she died, she was making pancakes for dinner. But we were out of syrup. He offered to go get it, but she insisted he stay and have more time with me." He starts crying again, his face like that of a scared little boy.

The same little boy I've seen glimpses of my whole life. Only now, I know who he is. I touch Daddy's knee, gently encouraging him to continue.

"He stayed with me the whole week. When he dropped me off at my grandmother's house after the funeral, he said he'd be back to get me. Said I'd come live with him. Even left me with a set of keys to what was supposed to be my new house. But he never came back."

"Oh my gosh. I'm so sorry," I say, feeling way down deep in his sadness. The tears that have been gathering in my eyes fall down my cheeks.

"No, I'm sorry. I've ruined everything. But I wanted you to know the truth," he says, and hangs his head.

I wipe my face. Wait, does he think bringing me here and telling me all of this will somehow let him off the hook with telling me about Shannon? I know he hurts more than I ever knew, but I still need answers. "What about Shannon? Why did you keep her a secret? Who's her mother? Where did you meet her? How long was the affair? What do you do when you see Shannon every Sunday? Didn't you feel bad for lying to us? For keeping her from us? How could you?" All my questions come flying out all at once, scared that if they wait, they won't get answers.

He looks up but doesn't say anything.

"Sorry, that didn't come out the way I wanted it to. But I need to know."

"Oh, Angel-face," he says, a big tear falling down his right cheek. "Of course, I feel bad. I hate myself for what I've done," he says, and hangs his head for way too long.

"Come on, now," I say, trying not to get mad all over again.

"Okay. Amanda, Shannon's mom, was my neighbor and best friend throughout high school. She was the only one who knew the truth about Mommy and my father. I used to connect with her on Facebook. Then one day we met up for lunch. Then we met up again. I don't even know what happened, and then she got pregnant."

Oh, I know what happened, I think, but keep my mouth shut so he keeps talking.

"After I found out, I told myself I would tell your mom. Then days passed, months passed, and Shannon was born. And every day afterward, I kept begging myself to tell. Then years passed and the lie got so big . . . and you and Cole were getting so big. It killed me to think how much it would disappoint you. I felt so . . . so ashamed. What would people think? And I knew your mom would never forgive me. I didn't want to lose my family. I couldn't lose my family," he says, tears coming down fast and hard.

I feel sorry for him. Sorry for the part of him who's still that hurt little boy. Mostly sorry that the little boy is still there, hurting. Sorry that after all these years, Daddy still hasn't learned how to heal him.

But I'm still pissed. At all his lies, his betrayal of Mom . . . of our family. Even at how he treated Shannon. I can't imagine how knowing you're a secret child must feel. So much of what my dad did is messed up. So much of my dad is messed up.

How am I his daughter and know better than he does? It's not normal. I swear it's like we're in some kind of twisted world where our roles are reversed, where I must grab his hand and pull him along, even though it's not my job. "Well, you can't keep Shannon in hiding anymore. We have to get to know her," I say, not believing my own words. "And you need to tell Cole."

ALL

UP

IN

IT

● REX ●

In the car my father asks, "So, what's going on with Carli?"

I turn my head and eye him like, *Why you all up in mine?* but he's too focused on the road to notice. I'm really not used to him being in my business like this. All week he's been coming into my room, asking me about this or wanting to know that, I guess trying to have more of a relationship. I mean, in theory it's what I want, too, but dude, can we ease into it?

"Not much," I answer. I really don't want to talk about Carli. I already think about her enough. Every time I see a girl with big hair or a girl wearing jean shorts or leggings or Nikes or a thin gold chain. Don't even let me walk by a hedge of jasmine (nothing on Earth smells as good as Carli's hair). I can't even get a T-shirt out my drawer without thinking about her. Or go outside in the woods behind the house. Or blow my own nose. Basically, I can't do shit. It's like my mind isn't even mine anymore.

"You talked to her since last Saturday?" My father is exiting at Old Spanish Trail off Highway 288. To the right is the Houston Zoo and the Texas Medical Center and to the left is our old neighborhood. *Where is this man taking me?*

I asked him this morning when he came into my room talking about going somewhere, but all he said was "Just come on." Normally, I wouldn't let that fly. I mean, you gotta tell me *something*. But this morning I was happy to roll out. You see, I usually hoop Saturday mornings, but I haven't been able to bring myself to touch a basketball since the championship. I'm not ready to face the game without my dream of going to the league.

"Yeah, briefly. We broke up," I reply.

He puts on his left turn signal and looks in his left-wing mirror. My father is about as careful as careful gets when it comes to driving. Every move so precise, like he's performing surgery or something. He finally takes a left on OST. Now we're passing the corner store

I used to ride my bike to for chips and soda. "I thought you said you really loved her."

Where the hell did that come from? It's like he's speaking on her behalf. Like she's somehow managed to possess his mouth like she's possessed my mind. "I do . . . I did," I say, all worked up. "But I'm trying not to."

"Okay, okay. Sorry, wasn't trying to pry," he says.

If that's not a lie, I think, but stay quiet, satisfied with him dropping it.

He takes a right on Scott Street, past a big, new stucco house under construction. The streets are poppin'. So many people out and about. We ride by three old men sitting on the porch of a pale-green, wooden house on blocks. Two little girls with pigtails trying to share a scooter on the sidewalk. Four dudes in a grassy driveway—two crouched down looking at something on a motorcycle and the other two eyeballing us as we roll by.

I'd forgotten how much my old neighborhood feels like a real community. How neighbors actually come out of their houses and talk to each other . . . even rely on one another. Man, the woman next door used to drop her little girl off with Angie all the time when her babysitter was running late and she had to be at work. And I don't know how many times the old man on the other side of the house asked us to help jump-start his pickup. And this one time when my father forgot to pay the water bill, the dude who lived behind us let me hook up a hose to his house for a couple days. I always talk about missing my old house, but I've missed this neighborhood, too.

My father takes a left on Luca and parks.

I might be glad to be back in the old hood and all, but I don't know why he would he bring me back to our old house. Did he see me sign up for the TV show where you knock on some stranger's door, tell them you used to live there, and ask if you can take a look around? No, I don't think so.

"Come on," he says, and gets out of the car.

I stay put.

A few moments later, he's standing in the middle of these people's freshly cut yard, waving for me to follow.

Nah, dude. You can have that. I keep my seat belt on. The house still looks the same: dark blue-gray paint with white trim. White mailbox near the front door hanging crooked, like it always has. I tried to straighten it out once, but my dad stopped me. He didn't say why, but Angie told me later that my mom had put it up.

Now my father's standing at the front door, looking back at me.

I look back at him but still don't take off my seat belt.

He turns away from me and slides a key into the lock.

Huh?

Now he's inside. And he left the door open.

The house has all the old furniture that my father said he donated to the Salvation Army. Plus, there are side tables and pillows and chairs and paintings and photographs and masks and jars and bowls and platters and pretty pencils and matches and things . . . lots of things I've never seen before. The living room has a whole new wall of records and books. *A Love Supreme* is sitting in an old record player, same as the one in my room.

I walk over to the breakfast room, which looks like someone's been working in it. There's an unfinished painting of a blue bird hanging on an easel and a mug full of paintbrushes sitting on the table next to a palette.

"There was a whole storage unit full of stuff I couldn't bring myself to get rid of," my father says, standing in the kitchen. I can only see the middle section of his body. The rest of him is hidden behind upper and lower rows of pale teal-painted cabinets.

I walk around the breakfast room and into the kitchen. "Is this all of Mom's old stuff?"

"Yeah," he says, his hope for my approval tangled in his voice.

As much as I love the idea of being surrounded by Mom's old things, him saving and arranging it all as if she's still living here isn't right. I walk toward him. "Dad," I say, feeling the newness of the word on my tongue. "Dad," I repeat, mostly because I like the way it feels.

He must see that I don't approve because his eyes tear up and his face flattens into what I recognize as shame—familiar in the most terrible way.

"Dad," and I wrap my arms around him. It feels weird at first, but I force myself to hold him and keep holding him until it doesn't feel weird anymore. Hold him and keep holding him until I can feel my anger for the ways he's wronged me start to seep out. "I think we should sell the house."

CARLI

It's Saturday afternoon and I'm lying on the sofa in the living room, trying not to feel the ghost of Rex (his arms around me, my face sunk into his neck) or the nothingness of my walls (its weight like concrete on my chest) by slipping further down into the YouTube abyss.

I'm home alone. Better than being at work with Mom. She tried to get me to go with her this morning, to get me out of the house, but I'm tired of looking into her sympathetic eyes. And I swear to god I'll go apeshit if I hear *Are you okay?* one more time.

Better than playing basketball with Jordan, too. After I told her about Shannon, she forgave me. But now all she wants to do is ball. Says she needs to step up her game since I'm not playing next year.

And definitely better than being at Daddy's. He's supposed to have *the talk* with Cole. No need for me to go through all that again.

I've been watching random videos for over three hours. So long I swear I can hear my brain yelling, *Help! Get me out of here!* And I'm trying, but "The World's Funniest Family Feud Fails" is putting all ladders and ropes out of my reach.

Steve Harvey is standing between two women, both with one hand behind their backs and the other hand flat on their respective red buzzers. He says, "Name a number that all men exaggerate."

Not the number of extramarital kids they have, I think before the lady in the purple dress presses the button and answers, "One hundred!" A red *X* flashes on the screen and Steve Harvey confusedly points to the other lady, who says, "Sixty-nine?"

I mean, how stupid can they be. I swear these women are even more clueless than me. I seriously didn't think that was possible. No, I take that back. Daddy is definitely more lost than I am. He's like a five-year-old trying to read a road map.

I go off hunting for the boost, the boost I thought judging Daddy would give me, but there isn't one. There's only his history—of being an eight-year-old boy whose mom died and whose dad never came back, of being a man who had a family and lost it—and the path stretched out before him.

I try to imagine my path, but all I see is a large stretch of earth covered with green, untrampled grass.

That does it. Phone down. I'm up. Stretching my long arms out to both sides and arching my back. Rex's strong hands around my waist. His thumbs gently rubbing my ribs. And I pull my arms in, look for another distraction, something that might stop me from remembering the feeling of his long body lying next to mine under the tall pines.

Magazines. A stack of them in the brass tray on the ottoman in the middle of the room. *Don't even think about it,* I tell myself. I'd be trying to cut out stuff for my walls in no time.

Books. Rows and rows of them that stretch floor to high ceiling on the wall at the foot of the sofa. But reading truths about other people's lives always makes me wonder about the truths of my own. And I'd only end up with some kind of quote I'd want to tack up on my walls.

My bare walls.

Just thinking about them makes this oversized burnt-orange sofa feel like my forever home. When I used to step into my room, a ton of images and poems and quotes and facts would greet me. Little bits of everything I loved. Little things that gave me a way to look at my life . . . at all the possible meanings for my feelings . . . at all the possible signs for which way to go.

But when I'm in there now (which is only when I'm getting dressed in the morning . . . I've been sleeping on the sofa all week), there is nothing but me.

But who am I, really? Without basketball. Without all the little things that I thought made up who I was. And if I don't even know who I am, how am I supposed to know what to do with the rest of my life. Can somebody please tell me that?

I'm so tired of trying to figure it all out. But even more tired of being out here, hiding. Hiding doesn't do anything but make your problems worse. I guess Daddy's mess taught me that.

No more hiding, I decide, and take a step toward the hallway. And another one, my long bare feet marching off the thick, woven rug onto the wooden floor. One after the other after the other until I'm standing at my closed bedroom door, yellow light shining on the tips of my toes.

I go in.

Even though I know what to expect, seeing my bare walls still feels like death. I look back at the black box holding all of my old things, buried under magazines in the corner of my closet crammed full of clothes. Knowing that they're there, that I can still visit them, is at least some kind of comfort.

When I turn back around, I notice that the afternoon light flooding my room is creating shadows on my walls. The far wall has one of the whole window: sixteen slanted, golden squares. Something. Not nothing. I go sit across from it on the edge of my made-up bed.

Jagged shadows running through a few of the glowing squares make me look outside of my window at a small tree. Its branches are covered with tiny green buds on their way to being leaves. So many buds. I count the ones on a single twig. Twenty-one. On another one. Seventeen. And another one. Twenty-four.

Don't ask me why, but it feels nice counting. Moving from one bud to the next with no thoughts in between. It's making me feel more alive than I've felt all week. Until it brings me to thinking about Rex.

It's not horrible to think about Rex. Even after what he did, so many memories of him still feel good. But some literally make me sick. Like that look of hate on his face at the championship game, and how he never even listened to what I had to say. How could he— *Wait, why am I even thinking about this?*

I grab my notebook and pencil off my desk and turn my attention back to the twigs outside the window. Make a mark for every green bud I count. Draw a leaf for every ten buds. A hundred buds and counting.

But then I start to wonder why the buds are taking so long to become full-grown leaves (it's already mid-March).

And that leads me to thinking that maybe the buds are a sign. That maybe I'm like the buds, growing slowly. *But into what? I need to know.*

But I don't, so I go back to counting. Until all the buds begin to blur, and I feel like I should go outside and start tagging the twigs I've counted to keep track. But nobody's doing all that. So I turn back to the glowing squares and think about how there are sixteen of them and sixteen years in me. How it could mean— *No, not going down that road again.*

I start sketching the squares instead—eyeing the correct angle of their slant, erasing and smudging to create the glow effect. I sketch and sketch, until the weight of trying to figure out what everything means and what I'll do with my life falls away. Until there is only the pencil, the paper, and the image I'm bringing into being.

Maybe this is who I am, right here where this pencil meets the page, where my eyes meet these glowing squares. So basic, I know, but the lightness, the wholeness, I feel right now is telling me there's something to it. Not the sketching itself, but me totally doing it, this one small thing. Giving all of my attention to it is letting me be.

● REX ●

I'm in the living room, on the opposite end of the sofa from my dad, trading cool home design pictures via IG. I didn't even have to sign him up. He already had an account. One of those zero posts, no profile pic accounts, but still. Who knew?

"Look at this one," he says from the other end of the sofa, his big feet in white socks almost reaching mine.

"Okay, give me a sec," I say, eyeing the image of a black heart with a jagged line going down the middle that just popped up on my feed. Another post from Cole. I swear Cole has posted over twenty times today.

Not his usual portraits, which always seem to reveal the unseen parts of people. Nah, it's a whole bunch of I'm-going-through-some-shit-type posts like, *Don't trust anyone* or *I remember when life was good* or *How can one person tell so many lies* or *The saddest thing about betrayal is that it never comes from your enemies.*

That girl with the slick-back ponytail and the wide-open eyes must've done him real dirty. He's been posting about her like crazy the last few weeks. And now this. I thought about texting him earlier, but I was scared he wouldn't want to hear from me after what I did to Carli. But this public breakup stuff has been going on for way too long. I'm not only worried about him, I'm starting to feel embarrassed for him.

You alright? I DM him on IG.

He hits me right back. **My dad is a fraud**

I look at my dad on the other end of the sofa. He's nowhere near perfect, but he's trying his best. I message back, **He's probably doing his best**

"Did you see the last one I sent?" my dad asks.

I click on the chat with my dad and see a picture of an all-white living room with a long, gray sofa and sleek, dark wood furniture. "Nah, this is basically the same look we have now. Not comfortable enough. And not enough color," I say, and look around.

I pause on the wall of windows that extend all the way from the kitchen into the living room. Outside a darkening orange-pink sky hovers over the pines. I was trippin' before. Our house is sick. It's this cool modern house with these huge windows that bring all the trees it's surrounded by in. But we still need help making it feel like a home.

"The sofa looks way more cushiony than ours," he says.

"It's still gray."

He laughs, says, "Okay, okay," and returns to his phone.

I click back on the conversation with Cole. He hasn't written anything after my last message. I wonder what happened with his dad. Damn, I didn't even ask.

What's going on with your dad? I text.

U don't know?

No

U haven't talked to Carli?

Not about your dad, I type, wondering if he even knows we've broken up.

The three little bubbles telling me he's typing appear then disappear, appear, then disappear.

I hop over to *Barbara A*'s feed and shoot my dad a pic of a white, modern living room with colorful art and a sunken middle floor filled with bright blue velvet cushions. "Now this is what I'm talking about," I tell him.

"Let me see," he says. And then, "Now that's nice."

"Carli's mom did it."

"Carli's mom, huh?" he says, like he's trying to sniff something out.

I see what he's getting at, but it's not how it looks. "Carli's mom's design style is dope. Only showing you. This has nothing to do with me and Carli, okay," I say, setting him straight.

"Yeah, okay."

I check Cole's conversation again and see, **Shannon's our sister. My dad cheated on my mom and kept Shannon a secret all these years**

WHAT??!!! I message back, not processing what I just read. It's too much to take in. **Dude, I'm so sorry. Are you okay?** I want to ask who Shannon is but don't. The name sounds familiar, but I can't place it.

I HATE MY DAD

I know he doesn't mean that, but I respond, **Man I can't even imagine,** and look at my dad. Although I spent a good deal of my life thinking he hated me, I've never hated him. And trust me, I've tried. I don't even know if it's possible to really hate someone you came from.

How do you look your wife in the face? Your kids? Like EVERY DAY for 15 YEARS knowing u have another child? Who does that?

I don't know man. That's sooooo messed up. I'm so sorry

And the crazy thing is that if Shannon hadn't told Carli during the game we still wouldn't know. He was trying to take it to the grave

Shannon? Oh shit! Shannon! That's what happened to Carli at the game! That's why she was so upset. The night flashes back to me, and I can almost tell the exact moment she must've found out. When she went from draining everything, including threes, to letting Shannon take over.

What! Are you serious?! I message back.

Said he was afraid to tell us. Such a punk. Can't even look at him the same. Can't wait to get out of this house

Want me to come scoop you?

Actually my girl just pulled up outside. Gotta go

OK . Call me if you need anything

Thx. Will do

"Sent you another one from her site," my dad says.

"Huh?"

"*Barbara A*. She's really good."

"Yeah?"

"I was just saying I sent you another photo from her site."

I know he means *feed*, but I don't correct him. I'm too busy thinking about Carli. I can't even imagine what she's been going through. She tried to tell me, but I refused to listen. I could've been there for her, but all I did was break up with her on top of everything else she had to deal with. And all because she missed my game? My game is nothing compared to what she found out. Nothing!

I swear I hate myself. No, I take that back. Talking shit about myself has way too much power. But why didn't I listen to her? I close my eyes and shake my head, wishing I could press Rewind, go all the way back to the game, calm my ass down, and wait to hear from Carli. But there are no do-overs. Only what I can do now.

"What's wrong? You don't like it? Ignore the pink sofa. I was referring to the overall look."

"No, no. It's not that," I say, standing up, knowing I'm too late. But I take off running toward the stairs and up to my room to call Carli anyway. Too late is for damn sure better than never.

CARLI

After the sun goes low and the shadows disappear from my walls, I bust out my colored pencils and sketch some heavily cratered moons, a few blazing suns, and a ton of tiny stars around and throughout the pencil-sketched squares.

Then I allow myself to thumb through a magazine, where I find Sabina Karlsson and cut out her face and big, red hair. I place the bottom third of her face underneath a moon, her freckled chin disappearing off the page. The left side of her face to the right, between a sun and some bud-filled branches. And her right eye and big red hair at the top among the stars.

Make her a part of everything, one piece at a time.

I even have the nerve to allow myself to bust out some books of poetry and look for passages that speak to me. Not so I can try to figure out what they mean for my future (that was driving me crazy), but so I can experience what they make me feel right now. And because I love the act of doing it. Come to think of it, I've always loved hunting through pages and writing my favorite passages down in my prettiest handwriting.

From Tracy K. Smith's *Life on Mars*, I write:

everything
That ever was still is, somewhere

Something about the passage makes me feel like I'm okay. Like everything will be okay. I draw a speech bubble around the passage, across three squares in the middle of the page, and listen. I hear a faint ring. Dang, what does that mean? Wait, I'm trippin'. That's my phone.

I get up and run down the hall to the living room, but it stops ringing before I get there. I grab my phone off the sofa and see a missed call from Rex. I want to roll my eyes, but before I can, my heart starts spinning then leaping then going still like it doesn't know what to do with itself.

A text from him pops up: **Talked to Cole. Sorry about your dad. I can't even imagine what you've been going through. Sorry I didn't listen. I should've listened. I hope you can forgive me. And I hope you're okay. You don't have to call me back. I just wanted you to know how sorry I am**

With his words floating around inside me, tears flood my eyes. I read his text ten more times, and a million thoughts rush in.

Does his apology mean that he wants to get back with me? If so, what was that whole you-don't-have-to call-me-back business? Is he trying to play games? Maybe not, but he's still messed up. But what do I really know? I know he loved me. I know I didn't really give him a fair chance. I didn't even tell him anything going on with me and expected him to understand. That's still no excuse for what he did. But he said he's sorry. I wonder if he still loves me. Is love enough?

All this thinking about Rex is taking me far, far away from myself. And after finally being so close, I want to hold on tight for a little longer. I want to go back to my bare room, sit on my bed, and listen for the words to go in my speech bubble. And afterward, hunt for more images from magazines. Oooo, maybe some lava or a blazing blue fire or something fiery red or maybe even something beige. I'll know it when I see it.

But definitely more sketches around whatever images I find, and a fact or two or three or four. And I don't know what else. I just want to keep at it long enough to know that I'll always be here.

Sounds crazy, I know. Like, where else am I going? But this just-being thing I have going on with myself is new. And between dealing with thoughts and emotions and decisions and plans and parents and siblings and boyfriends, I need to be able to trust that I can always get away from the world and back to just being myself.

I look down at Rex's text. The only thing I know for sure about him, about us, right now is that I appreciate him apologizing. It makes the part of me that feels wronged by him want to close its case. **Thanks for texting . . . I'm okay**, I write back, and toss my phone on the sofa.

Above it, a waxing gibbous moon glows in the just-dark sky outside the window. I stand still for a while and take it in, resisting the urge to think about what the moon means for me and Rex, resisting the urge to think about anything.

NOTHING
AND
EVERYTHING

● REX ●

Saturday morning and I'm crouching down in the mudroom, lacing up my LeBrons, when my phone pings. Man, I hope it's Carli. It's a stupid hope—when a girl thanks you for texting her, it's pretty much a nice way of saying she's done with your ass—but I allow myself to have it anyway.

I mean, maybe she misses me. I know I miss her. It's been a week since I've texted, but it feels like a lifetime. Nah, make that seven lifetimes because every day that passes without talking to her feels like a new death. But I'm trying not to bother her about us when she's dealing with so much else.

I stand up and dig my phone out of the pocket of my basketball shorts. **Still on?**—a text from Cole. He asked me to meet him up at the secret court today. He's spending the weekend at his dad's and wants to get out of the house. I definitely get that.

You know it, I text back. **Heading up there now**. I'd planned to go up there today anyway. Been going all week after school, too, since Coach is still too pissed to open the gym for me.

Yep, I'm back to ballin'. I figure to hell with what everybody is saying about me. What they think won't get me any closer to my dream. Yes, your boy's dream is still alive! Can't let it die. Shit, nobody's ever accomplished anything without trying. And I'm telling you, now, I'm about to put in work. Major work.

I thought we said 2, Cole replies.

Yeah, going early to get some shots in

Dang, I ◉◉ u

Ha! I'm trying!

Below Cole's conversation is a conversation with Danny. He texted to invite me to a party he's having tonight. Said his parents were out of town for the weekend and he was getting kegs. Been to enough white-boy wasted parties (one) to know it's not my thing, but I plan to go anyway. Can't pass up the opportunity to try to smooth things over with the team.

Below the conversation with Danny, Carli's message of

thanks still sits, staring at me like a hand up in my face. I swear every time I see it, all the air rushes out my lungs.

This can't be the end of us.

I type, **Miss you**, and erase it. **Miss you** again and press Send before I can lose my nerve. Maybe she's done with me, maybe she's not. But how will I ever know if I don't start trying to fix what I've messed up.

CARLI

I'm driving back to Daddy's from my Photoshop class at HCC. Missed the first class of the session last Saturday, but I still killed it. And I was afraid I was going to be too far behind . . . afraid I wasn't going to be as good as those college kids. Chile, please! The teacher even said he was impressed by me.

Let me back up. After basically spending all last week filling up my notebook with sketches and quotes and facts and magazine clippings—each page with a totally different look, giving a completely different feel—I realized I was pretty good at collage.

Sounds crazy, I know. I've basically been doing it on my

walls since I was a kid. But I always thought putting random things together in interesting ways would eventually tell me what I really wanted to do with my life. I never considered the possibility that it could actually be the thing I do. Duh!

And even when the possibility first popped in my head, I was still like, *A collage artist? Me? Nooo.* But I am. Not to say that it's all I'll ever be. Maybe it will be, and I'll just keep getting better and better. Or maybe it will lead to something else I love. Or maybe I'll end up doing something completely different with my life.

All I know is that right now, I want to take my collage skills to the next level. I want to learn how to do it digitally. Where it takes me, who knows? But getting better at something I love feels like a step in the right direction. And that's all I can ask for.

Plus, it will keep me out of the house on the Saturdays I have to spend at Daddy's. Oh, I forgot to tell you: the judge decided that I'll live with Mom during the week and Cole will live with Daddy. I still don't know how I'm going to live without Cole, but at least we'll be together on the weekends—first and third at Daddy's and second and fourth at Mom's. If there's a fifth weekend, we get to choose where to spend it.

Anyway, it's not like I'm still *that* mad at Daddy, but all he wants to do now is cry and apologize and explain the same things over and over again. It's like listening to the same sad song on repeat. A sad song that's not about to fix anything.

Pulling up to the house, I see Jordan's Jeep in the driveway beside Daddy's Tahoe. She beat me here. I had to beg her to skip ballin' today to come over here to be my backup. Figure things can't get too depressing with company around.

Walking up the driveway, I notice the magnolia tree is better. It has way less of that nasty white stuff on its limbs. Whatever the tree guy sprayed on it must be working. Makes me want to fish my phone out of my backpack and send Rex a pic, but I don't.

Got his text this morning—**Miss you**—and I swear I could feel him whispering it in my ear. But I'm in such a good place with myself. Don't know if I'm ready to risk that by starting things back up with Rex. Plus, I don't know if I can ever really trust him again.

Jordan thinks I should give him another chance. I think her exact words were, *Yo ass act like you've never messed up.* And I haven't even told her about his latest text yet. No doubt she's about to give me a hundred reasons to call him back. I grab the gold door handle—warm from the sun—push the latch down with my thumb, and press open the door, already hearing some of the reasons.

Now I can't hear anything. I can only see Shannon. Yes, old-enemy-new-sister Shannon. I know I told Daddy that we needed to get to know her, but I didn't expect to come back today and see her standing in the living room. Cole is giving her a hug.

Cole lets go of her and they both look over at me. Daddy, standing beside them, looks at me. Jordan, half-swallowed by the sofa, looks at me, too. Everyone's eyes are red and glossy like they've been crying, including Jordan's. And Jordan doesn't cry.

"Hey," I say, feeling like I'm not even here, like this isn't real.

"Hey," they say, voices dragging. No one even tries to fake a smile. Boy, was I wrong about things not getting too depressing with company around.

This has to end. It would be different if these were finally-united-and-it-feels-so-good tears. That would actually be nice. But tears from another stop on Daddy's apology tour? Nobody has time for that. I'm mad Jordan had to sit in on it. This heaviness is not hers. Really, it's not any of ours. It's Daddy's.

"It's super nice outside. Y'all wanna go up to the basketball court?" I ask, hardly believing the words coming out of my mouth. But dribbling and shooting under the sun would be way better than staying here in this funk.

Brighter faces all around. Except for Daddy's. He's looking down at the floor, his mind somewhere else.

Jordan climbs out of the sofa. "Hadn't planned on ballin' today, but you know I'm always down." She's wearing her Jordan 9 Retros. She doesn't usually ball in her Retros.

"I thought ballin' was always the plan," Shannon says, and bites the nail on her pointer finger. She's dressed in a baggy T-shirt, long shorts, and some Nike Dunks—clearly ready.

"Plan?" I look at Daddy, but he's still looking down at the floor. Then I look at Cole. His long, lightly freckled cheeks are going pink. Of course it was Cole. But you know what? I can't even be mad.

Shannon is our sister. Like, I have a sister. And she's real. She's standing in our living room with chewed-up nubs for nails (does she know how many hundreds of thousands of bacteria can live under just one dirty nail?) and her hair tied back in a bun. Wait, did she tie it back for me? I need to tell her she doesn't have to do that. I need to tell her so many things.

I mean, I'd be lying if I said Shannon being here doesn't feel strange. But it feels more normal than when I first walked in. And I'm sure it will feel even more normal when we get out of this house. Will it ever feel completely normal having a sister I only learned about at sixteen? I don't know. But life isn't about to sit around and wait on normal.

● REX ●

Carli just walked through the opening in the hedges. No. Can't be. But the way the sun is glinting off the gold medallion on her chest, and the way her big hair is bouncing off her bare shoulders, tell me I'm not trippin'.

She's walking behind Cole—and wait, is that Shannon?—rockin' some high-top yellow Blazers with a tank top and some cut-off jean shorts. And now Jordan just walked in, too. Cole never said anybody else was coming.

Man, but Carli. I wasn't prepared to see her today. I swear to God I'm so happy I could cry. All I want to do is run to her and scoop her up in my arms. But I know I don't have the right. And the face she's making isn't giving me any type of permission.

You'd think that when every picture you've ever looked at of a person, and everything you've ever done with a person, constantly plays like reruns in your brain, that you would've seen every face they could possibly make. But this one is new.

She's looking straight at me . . . like what? Dude, I don't know. Definitely no smiling or sweetness going on. Probably too much to ask. But no anger or attitude, either. At least I could've worked with that. Normally when girls get mad, that means they still care. But Carli's face is straight-up blank, like she doesn't feel anything.

I drop the ball at the free-throw line and walk toward her, hoping to see something I'm missing.

CARLI

When I see Rex on the court, I swear the sun turns up a notch. It's like my world literally got brighter.

But should I be feeling this? I look back at the sidelines, at the shade along the chain-link fence with the tall, green bushes poking through. It looks so tempting. I could go sit down, lean back, and wait for some kind of sign to tell my confused heart what to do.

But I don't. I keep walking, putting one yellow Blazer (they're new) in front of the other on the green court. I wonder what it's made of. It's a lot softer than concrete, that's for sure.

Ahead of me, Cole gives Rex a hug. Then Shannon awkwardly hugs him, too, like she doesn't know what else to do. Jordan runs ahead of me, daps him up, and tries to beat Shannon to the ball.

My turn.

REX

How I've missed her little nose, her quiet brown eyes, and her fierce freckles. They snatch me up, pull me in, and I get lost inside.

CARLI

Being this close to Rex has my heart speaking in colors again. A kingdom of colors. Making all the arguments for our love that words and thoughts couldn't come up with. It's such an unbelievably good feeling. Like my heart just gave birth to it. Like I've never felt it before.

But I have.

And as much as I want to let the feeling carry me away, cocoon me in all the colors, I can't. Not yet. For now I feel safer with things being beige.

REX

"Hi," I say, my eyes moving from the patch of freckles on her nose up to her eyes.

"Hi," she says, her eyes resting on mine, but somehow not giving me anything.

"I'm really sorry for what I did to you," I start. "I was just—"

"Wait, can we not do this?"

Damn, she doesn't even want to hear my apology? She's really done with me. But she doesn't even know that I've been working on myself. I need her to know. "Can I at least apologize?"

"You already did."

"But it's different in person."

"Yeah, but the sun is shining. And the sky is so blue. We're here. Back at the secret court. It's so soft," she says, and hops up and down a little bit. "I can't believe I didn't notice this the last time we were here."

I really don't know what's going on right now, but I hop up and down a little, too, try to see what sees talking about. I guess it's got a little spring to it. "Yeah, much better than concrete."

"Exactly," she says, staring at me.

I can't think of anything else to say, so I don't say anything.

And neither does she.

We stay like that for a while, and I finally see what her eyes are giving me. They're here . . . she's here . . . right now . . . with me. And I swear it feels like we're out of our skin. Like there's nothing covering us. Nothing in the way.

It's the best feeling in the world, but I can't even lie, it's making me feel kind of shy. "So, Shannon is here," I say, and turn to look back at everybody else. Shannon grabs the rebound from Cole's missed shot before Jordan does.

"Yeah, Cole set it up."

"Gotta love Cole."

"Yeah, I'm pretty sure he set this up, too," she says, and twists her lips. But her eyes have the happiness of a thousand smiles. Okay, maybe not a thousand but at least one.

"Looks like it," I say, a monument of hope springing up inside of me.

"So how are we about to do this?" Cole yells over to us. "We got five. Quick game of horse to see who sits out first?"

"No, y'all go ahead. I'm not playing," Carli yells back.

Takes everybody a second to process, but then Jordan finally shouts, "Damn, that's right!"

CARLI

Didn't feel like sitting on the sidelines. Wanted to be in the mix with everybody else, so I'm the ref. Just called Cole for his third foul on Rex.

"You've gotta be kidding me!" Cole complains, throwing his hands up in the air from the baseline. "You're clearly giving Rex preferential treatment. I can't even look his direction without you calling a foul."

"Yeah, you can't be out here playing favorites if you're the ref," Shannon backs him up from the middle of the key. Didn't take her any time to get comfortable with sibling bickering.

"Nobody's playing favorites," I snap back, and grab the ball from underneath the basket. "It's not my fault y'all haven't found a way to guard him yet. Stay in front of him. Keep a hand in his face. Block him out so he doesn't keep getting all the rebounds."

"Oh, so now you're the ref and the coach?" Cole replies.

"Tell me about it!" Shannon echoes.

I dribble the ball a few times, noticing how it pops up quicker than it would on a normal court. "Whatever. Don't be mad at me. I'm just callin' it like I see it."

"Y'all are funny," Jordan says, and walks to the low block.

Rex walks to the free-throw line, looking uncomfortable with being in the middle of all the arguing.

"Oh, I almost forgot," Jordan says, turning toward me. She reaches into her sneakers and pulls out a piece of paper rolled up into a flattened scroll. "Here," she says, and holds it out.

"Ew, I'm not touching that," I reply.

"Girl, would you look," she says, eyes wide, and unrolls it. The hospital menu.

I quickly slide the ball between my left elbow and hip and take it. The paper is damp from Jordan's sweaty feet, but I don't care. I flip it over, and there it is in blurred blue ink:

The very first kisses were blown in Mesopotamia as a way to get in good with the gods.

Tangible evidence of where it all began for me and Rex. A sign of where we're going? Maybe, but who has time to try to figure that out?

Don't get me wrong. I'm not totally giving up on my signs. I still believe that if I pay attention, signs will pop up and let me know I'm on the right path. But all that business of thinking everything was a potential sign had to stop. Some things just are what they are, and trying to give them extra meaning all the time was overcomplicating my life.

Take me and Rex. Regardless of the first-kisses fact, our fate will depend on how we treat each other—how much of the good in ourselves we're willing and able to give each other—simple as that.

But should I at least give him the menu? So he can always have it as a reminder of how I've felt from the very beginning, no matter what happens to us?

"Any day now," Cole says, walking up to the block opposite Jordan.

Shannon sets up beside him, already looking ready to rebound even though Rex hasn't even shot his first free throw.

I bounce pass the ball to Rex with my right hand, still trying to decide what to do with the menu in my left.

Rex catches the ball and dribbles—one, twice, three times, and swish. No kisses.

I grab the ball and pass it back to him.

Again—once, twice, three times, and swish. No kisses.

The first time he went to the line and didn't blow a kiss, I thought he might've forgotten.

The second time I allowed myself to hope. That he'd stopped asking forgiveness from his mom. That he'd realized her death wasn't his fault. That he'd somehow let go of his pain and rearranged himself into a boy who would never hurt me again.

Now three times, and the hope in my chest slides on its wings and starts flapping all over the place. I can't help but think that there will be more between us. Much, much more.

But only the future knows.

I slide the menu into my back pocket, where I keep it for myself. And the game goes on. With us and only what belongs to us. Nothing else.

ACKNOWLEDGMENTS

Book two. *Say what?* I feel so incredibly grateful to be putting more words into the world. For me, writing has always been an exercise of going deep within, extracting bits of my human experience, and shaping them into a universal story. The fact that people are reading my stories and connecting to them feels so rewarding. So, to all my readers: thank you, thank you, thank you! You don't know how much you mean to me.

To my little family, Amina and Larry: you give my heart a home. A home filled with light and beauty and joy and kindness and peace. I'm so grateful to have you both. I love you.

Seneca Shahara Brand, aka Sha Love: I'm so lucky to have such a loving, artistic friend. Thank you for being so generous with your creative gifts. This book wouldn't be the same without you.

Rochelle and Stan, aka Mom and Dad: None of this would be possible without your continued love and support. Thank you. I love you.

Loveis Wise: I love your name. I love the energy you put into the world through your work. Thank you for putting that energy into this book's cover. It's gorgeous, and Carli and Rex are perfect.

To my agent, Jennifer Carlson: Thank you for being my advocate. I am happy I have you.

To my editor, Virginia Duncan, and everyone at Greenwillow Books/HarperCollins: thank you for turning my words into a book and getting that book out into the world.